Child of Light

A.S.Chambers

This story is a work of fiction.
All names, characters and incidents portrayed are fictitious and the works of the author's imagination. Any resemblance to actual persons, living or dead is entirely coincidental.

Copyright © 2024 Basilisk Books.

All rights reserved. No part of this publication may be reproduced, stored in a retrieval system, or transmitted, in any form or by any means without the prior written permission of the publisher, nor be otherwise circulated in any form of binding or cover other than that in which it is published and without a similar condition being imposed on the subsequent purchaser.

A.S.Chambers asserts his moral right to be identified as the author of this work.

Cover art © Artist Axentevlad

ISBN: 978-1-915679-63-5

Acknowledgements

For all my Patreon and Kickstarter supporters who helped my financially and emotionally in the creation of the book.

With special mention to the following:
Bec Pearce, Ron Chick, Lee Hardy, Rebecca Armstrong, Debs SteamGoth, Sharon R Farrimond, Charlie, Simon Brindley, Paul L, Melissa, Ariion Dragoa, Kevin Denwood, Jacob Matts and Gemma Innes.

Thank you, you wonderful readers!

Also, a huge thanks to Rachel Lowe for beta reading this outing of the Twins as well as Child of Fire.

Also by A.S.Chambers

Sam Spallucci Series.
The Casebook of Sam Spallucci – 2012
Sam Spallucci: Ghosts From The Past – 2014
Sam Spallucci: Shadows of Lancaster – 2016
Sam Spallucci: The Case of The Belligerent Bard – 2016
Sam Spallucci: Dark Justice – 2018
Sam Spallucci: Troubled Souls – 2020
Sam Spallucci: Bloodline - Prologues & Epilogue – 2021
Sam Spallucci: Bloodline – 2021
Sam Spallucci: Fury of the Fallen – 2022
Sam Spallucci: The Case of The Pillaging Pirates – 2023
Sam Spallucci: Lux Æterna – 2024

Short Story Anthologies.
Oh Taste And See –2013
All Things Dark And Dangerous – 2015
Let All Mortal Flesh – 2016
Mourning Has Broken – 2018
Hide Not Thou Thy Face – 2020
If Ye Loathe Me – 2022
Out of the Depths – 2023
Hear My Scare – Due 2025

Ebook short stories.
High Moon - 2013
Girls Just Wanna Have Fun – 2013
Needs Must - 2019

Novellas.
Songbird – 2019
Bobby Normal and The Eternal Talisman – 2021
Bobby Normal and the Virtuous Man – 2021
Bobby Normal and the Children of Cain – 2022
Bobby Normal and the Children of Cain – 2022
Bobby Normal and The Fallen – 2023
Bobby Normal and the Black Dragon – 2024
Child of Fire – Due 2025

Omnibuses.
Children of Cain - 2019
Macabre Collection: Volume One – 2022
Macabre Collection: Volume Two – 2023
Sam Spallucci Omnibus: Volume One – 2022
Sam Spallucci Omnibus: Volume Two – 2024
The Adventures of Bobby Normal – 2024

Contents

Chapter One	1
Chapter Two	13
Chapter Three	27
Chapter Four	45
Chapter Five	94
Chapter Six	134
Author's Notes	142
About The Author	147

Child of Light

Chapter One

The final day of my so-called normality began just as they all did back then.

"Come on. Get up. Time to kill."

I lay deathly still in my crumpled bedsheets, my eyes focused on the cracked white paint of the ceiling above. One of the cracks looked like a map of Ireland. From the pattern of spindly lines, a thin cobweb ran to the faded cable from which a beige lampshade was suspended. I think the silken strands had been there for at least six months. I had no idea where the spider was. I tried to hold my breath long enough to make myself pass out. I rationalised that, if I was unconscious, then perhaps the insidious voice would stop. Unfortunately, my respiratory system had other ideas and my treacherous lungs gasped inwards as my unseen tormentor chuckled quietly to himself.

"Go away," I muttered, barely audibly. The last thing that I wanted was for my parents to think I was cracking up.

Not that I think they would have noticed, to be fair.

"You can say that again, Bucko."

I grunted in frustration and swung my legs out from under my worn, tired bedding. Green, maniacally smiling frogs stared up at me from the soft material of the duvet cover, just as they had done every morning for the past ten years. There was a small tear along the mouth of one of the grinning amphibians where the ancient fabric had thinned. The duvet beneath was poking through, constructing the illusion of a warped, deformed tongue. Sitting on the edge of the bed, I first screwed my fists into my eye sockets to remove the nighttime sleep detritus then banged my knuckles on the sides of my head in a vain attempt to knock my lodger into unconsciousness.

"Now, you know that doesn't work. You'll just get a headache."

I caught the usual whiff of strong tobacco and wrinkled my nose in disgust. Neither my parents nor I smoked, so where did it come from every damned morning? After grabbing my clothes off the floor, I dragged them on so that they vaguely resembled a school uniform. Shambling out of my bedroom and thumping down the stairs, the strong smell of cigarettes trailed along beside me, an aromatic shadow.

I trudged into the kitchen and saw my mother busying herself chopping something with her large, green chef's knife — the one she'd bought from one of the varying shopping channels at which her dead eyes stared blankly all day. Those same heavy-lidded eyes were currently gazing down at the purple vegetable (An aubergine? I'm really no good at identifying anything apart from a carrot…) as the knife slid back and forth in its own repetitive motion.

The tobaccoey presence peered over my shoulder at the shell of a woman in front of me.

Child of Light

"Take the knife," it hissed into my ear. *"Snatch it from her hand. Stab her! See what happens. You'll be amazed."*

Perhaps I've got a brain tumour? I pondered, diverting myself away from the proffered form of matricide and, instead, grabbing an open box of cornflakes off the counter. *That could explain all this. Whatever this is...*

I began to eat the cereal straight from the box.

"Don't do that, Ally." My mother's voice was distant, listless. She didn't even turn around to scold me. She just continued to watch the knife in her hand as it rhythmically sliced through the purple vegetable in precisely measured intervals.

I shook my head and continued to eat my breakfast. "Don't call me Ally," I complained around mouthfuls of the most important meal of the day. "You know I don't like it. It's a girl's name."

"Okay, Ally," drifted back the lacklustre voice. "If you say so."

I rolled my eyes and consumed more cereal. Every morning was the same. Day in, day out. There was the voice, the smell, my mother, then...

"Morning, Champ!" My father bounded into the room, the perfect poster boy for whatever would put vim and vigour into your otherwise mundane life. His immaculate blue suit was fiercely pressed and a broadsheet newspaper was clamped firmly under his arm. He pecked his wife on her vaguely proffered cheek, tousled his son's dark, wavy hair, picked up his packed lunch and strode out of the house to a place of work that I neither knew the identity of nor cared a hoot about.

I stared down into the box of cereal; the cornflakes stared back up at me. That's what my parents were really, weren't they? Cornflakes. They looked like they belonged in the adverts, all middle class, smartly dressed and loving, but in reality, they were just tiny little fragments that could be turned to mush at the slightest drop of milk.

"You need to work on your metaphors..."

I frowned. Okay, so perhaps the analogy wasn't perfect. In fact, it was total rubbish. Just like my so-called life.

Ah, screw it, I thought to myself. *I'm going to school.*

To say that I hated school would most definitely be something of an understatement. I had the feeling that I was in fact serving out my time in purgatory for a wealth of sins and misdemeanours I had carried out in a previous existence. Perhaps I had been a cat that had eaten too many prize goldfish? Perhaps I had been a general that had led his troops into numerous pointless battles? Perhaps I had been a grinning, fake-tanned salesman on a banal shopping channel that sold stoned housewives crap they didn't need on a daily basis? It wasn't that school was *bad* as such. It was just decidedly *tedious*. The lessons came and went with the expected rhythm of a three-legged mammoth lurching to its ultimate death over the side of a very steep cliff. The teachers droned on and on about things that neither intrigued nor appealed to me. What did I need to know about the inner workings of the nervous system? Why should I care what led to Harold losing the battle of Hastings?

Dull, dull, dull, dull, dull.

And, to make matters worse, my lodger always seemed to have an opinion on everything.

"Why on earth would they think that Nero played a

Child of Light

fiddle?

"All that work on gravity and they just bang on about that stupid apple!

"So many words; so little meaning..."

The other issue was that it was so *noisy*. Now, I know that high schools aren't the most chill of places at the best of times; they're full of hormonal teenagers either crying over what they perceive to be the greatest tragedy on the planet or running down the corridors, quacking like a duck. No, what I mean is that it was noisy *in my head*.

To accompany the sarcastic mutterings of my disembodied lodger, there was a continual buzzing noise, like an angry wasps' nest. The more people there were around me, the more it grew in violent intensity. It would start ramping up as I walked to school, the trickle of other students gradually flowing into at first a stream, then a river, until I was awash in an immense ocean. It brewed up into a distracting, overwhelming tempest of sound that would crash in continual tsunamis upon the coastal towns and cities of my brain, crushing the tiny grey matter of buildings and drowning the synaptic residents. At break times, I would head over to the furthest corner of the school field and try to distance myself from my peers as much as possible. During my lessons, I would focus on blocking out the hubbub. I would imagine walls of cotton wool around me as mufflers to deaden the buzzing.

It took so much effort.

It was just so tiring.

So, by the end of the day, I would normally just sit at the back of the classroom, close my eyes and let the last hour of the day sweep past me. It was weird though, as I drifted internally, my mind swimming away from the dry, stuffy classroom, not once did my teachers ever notice that I was daydreaming. Not once did those around me ever dob me in or punch me in an attempt to ruin my pleasant dreams of escape. It was as if they thought that I was still alert and paying attention.

Or perhaps they just didn't see me there, escaping to somewhere far more pleasant?

Normally, I would choose somewhere secluded; a place where I could be completely alone. It might be a long, curving beach of baking hot sand or a dense, overgrown forest, with sunlight dappling the pleasantly fragrant floor. I would walk in solitary bliss, the screaming buzz of those around me in the real world momentarily quieted.

Today, though, the dream was different.

For once, I was not alone.

I was walking through dry, dusty streets that were full of people. It appeared to be a city composed of small, hand-fashioned dwellings. Huge oxen pulled wooden carts down the narrow streets and the inhabitants called out cheerfully to each other, some of them occasionally waving to me and my companion.

She was a girl, a young girl. She was about four or five and didn't look like the others in the town. They were all brown-skinned with jet-black hair, yet she was Caucasian, like me, but had flowing locks of blonde as opposed to my dark brown mop. Her fair hair was streaked with shots of vivid red, framing her deep brown eyes that seemed to burn brightly in the sunlight as she dragged me to a great river that flowed past our city, our home.

"Alec, look in the water," she said and I complied, bending over. In the gentle ripples of the river, I saw a face that was many years younger than it should be. I appeared to be a similar age to my companion. And, as I peered wonderingly at our reflections, the girl placed her small hand in the rapid current and then started to giggle as the water boiled and steamed at her touch. "Look!" she shrieked with glee. "Look what I can do."

Then I felt something stir inside my head, like the echo of a lilting voice reflecting off a rock face. "Mother is calling," I said. We got up and walked hand in hand back to our home where an adult version of the girl was standing with a warm smile twinkling from her eyes that matched mine, a bright blue.

And, as the three of us stood there, smiling warmly, enjoying this gentle domestic moment, I heard a heavy footfall behind me and the dark voice of my lodger growled, *"This never happened. You had it robbed from you. Snatched from your infant grasp. Your heart longs for this stolen reality."*

The dream, like all the others before it, faded. The class finished and I drifted out of the building, leaving the infernal hubbub behind, but taking something else with me.

Curious wonder.

I barely noticed the daily trudge home. One footstep must have successfully followed another as the scene from the daydream replayed continually on a loop in my head.

Who was the girl? Who was the woman that I had called our mother? Also, where had we been?

I eventually found myself on my front doorstep, my hand poised to press down on the worn, brass door handle. I gave the outside world one more quick glance. I watched passersby as they walked down the street and heard the buzzing inside my head, quieter now due to there being fewer people around.

I opened the door and stepped inside, closing it firmly shut behind me.

Blissful silence descended on me.

"And why do you think that might be?"

Well, almost silence.

"You're living a lie."

"Go away."

"This isn't you. You've seen what they took from you, what it should have been."

"This isn't real. I'm just tired."

"Is that you, Ally?" My mother's voice drifted over to me from the living room. "Have you brought a friend home?"

"No, Mum," I sighed, dragging myself upstairs and changing out of my uniform into jeans, a T-shirt and a grey, zip-up hoodie. I headed back down and walked into the living room.

My mother was sitting on the sofa, watching a pair of smiling phonies selling the latest, greatest kitchen gadget. "I could have sworn I heard you talking to someone," she said listlessly.

"You know I don't have any friends."

She didn't reply. Her eyes remained fixed on the flickering screen. Images of the plastic salespeople played out in front of her blank eyes.

The only sound I could hear right then was the sound of the programme.

"And why do you think that might be?" The same question again. *"Why can you hear the buzz of everyone else but not her?"*

I thought back to the constant suffocating babble in

the world outside my house. There wasn't a whisper of it here in this room. Perhaps I just imagined it? Perhaps I was tired? Perhaps I was going crazy? Let's face it, I had a voice in my head that certainly wasn't mine! What was next? Looking for hairs in the palms of my hands?

The images of the girl and my other mother drifted into my head and an overwhelming sense of belonging washed over me.

"Yes. That is what should have been real. This... This is an abomination. See her. Really see her..."

I stared at the middle-aged woman watching her stupid programme from her worn, faded sofa. I stared hard until my eyes watered.

"Don't use those eyes; use the ones inside your head."

I frowned but did as I was told. I took the image in front of me and stuck it in a black area inside my imagination, away from the distractions of the dull domestic life that surrounded me. As I did, it was as if something had been peeled away from my physical eyes, a filter that had been lain over the image of the woman had been removed.

In fact, it wasn't a woman at all!

There, sitting on the sofa of my living room, was a tall, brown monster. Its skin was smooth and rippled as its arms moved, long arms that ended in four sharp digits. Its head, an eyeless dome atop a trunk of a body, turned towards me and a long, slithering tongue flickered out between its wide lips. "Ally," grated a totally inhuman voice, "what's wrong?"

I took a step back and bumped into someone standing right behind me. Turning, I was confronted with a man dressed in a black denim jacket, dark glasses covering his eyes. "You have to kill it before it warns the others," he spoke in the familiar voice of my lodger. "Quickly!"

I darted out of the room and into the kitchen. On the draining board lay the green chef's knife that had been chopping a nameless purple vegetable just that morning. I snatched it up just as the creature lumbered in behind me. "Ally? What are you doing?" came the gurgling voice as it reached one of its deformed hands out towards me.

I lunged forwards and swung the knife down. Its grotesque, non-human hand dropped to the floor. The creature paused, stared at its stump, then vigorously shook the dismembered wrist as a new hand sprouted from the wound. Its head snapped back to face me and its mouth opened wide, the hideous tongue whipping out and lashing around my neck. Spots began to form in my vision as the tongue began to squeeze, dragging me across the floor to the monster. I hacked down with the knife and the beast squealed wetly as its black tongue split in two. Throwing myself at its chest, I plunged the blade deep into its torso. Reaching out, it picked me up and threw me casually across the kitchen. I rolled across the central counter and lay stunned against the back door, watching in horror as the monster wrapped its fingers around the hilt of the knife, pulling the weapon out of its chest with a wet schlupping sound.

My lodger walked casually into the room, glanced at the creature, then at me, before shaking his head. "Not like this. You can't kill constructs that way." He tapped the side of his head. "Reach out to it. Convince it to do the job for you."

I grimaced and frowned at the creature as it made its way purposefully around the counter. I focused on its head, where I guessed its brain to be. I reached out with my imagination, visualised a dark void within the creature, and I gripped it with make-believe hands. The creature paused mid-step and hissed. I squeezed harder and a high-pitched mewling sound emanated from its pursed lips. Its arms raised up and transformed from the four-fingered limbs into a pair of sharp blades. I squeezed even harder and the monster gave an agonised howl as it turned its limbs towards itself.

I pushed harder.

The blades swept down, slicing the beast into three parts, which collapsed onto the kitchen floor.

"Yes!" cheered the dark stranger. "That's my boy! Right, we have to leave. Now."

"Leave? What about my father?"

A dark eyebrow raised above the black sunglasses.

"Him too?"

He nodded.

I peered down at the three pieces of the monster. "Are they *moving*?"

"We'll need to work on your powers," the stranger muttered as he produced a packet of cigarettes out of his pocket and slipped one in between his lips. "For now, though, I'll finish off here." With that, he swept his right hand around in a flourish, producing a ball of fire in his palm. First, he bent over and ignited his cigarette, then he tossed the fire down at the pieces of the beast that had definitely begun to edge their way towards each other. I watched mesmerised as the flames seemed to dance of their own volition around the body parts, baking them hard, and I recalled the vision of the blonde girl making steam rise from the river.

I was snapped out of my reverie when the flames leapt from the monster to the wooden kitchen units.

"Okay, time to go!" The stranger walked casually through the growing flames. He placed his left hand on my shoulder and, with his right hand, clicked his fingers.

Child of Light

Chapter Two

We were no longer in my house. My heart was smashing against its ribcage prison, screaming for release, as my eyes scanned my new surroundings. It appeared to be an old cottage of some sort; a single-room affair. An ancient rocking chair listlessly swayed back and forth in one corner. A single, unmade bed was pushed up against the opposite wall. There was a sink, a table and a fireplace. Some remnants of food sat on a plate on the table. I pressed a tentative finger against a piece of bread. There was no give whatsoever.

My lodger was busying himself with arranging logs in an open fireplace. "You're shivering," he stated in a matter-of-fact manner. "I'm guessing it's shock. Come here and warm up. One of his hands reached out and the logs immediately burst into flame; the other beckoned to the rocking chair and it skittered across the wooden floor to his side. He held it steady. "Come, Alec. Sit."

I remained where I was and, instead of doing what he commanded, I studied him. He stood taller than me with dark hair similar to mine. His eyes were obscured behind the black sunglasses but I could feel them intently watching me. He wore black denim jeans and a black denim jacket over what looked to be a black t-shirt. I frowned as I noticed that he wore two badges on the jacket: one bore the CND emblem and the other said, "Prefect."

"Who the hell are you?" I forced out between chattering teeth.

"Alec…" He shook his head. "It's complicated. Dangerously complicated."

"That seems to be the story of my life now, though, doesn't it?"

He nodded and patted the back of the chair. "Please," he insisted, concern apparent in his voice, "sit. Before you fall dead on your feet. You've been through a lot."

I staggered to the chair and fell into its hard embrace. He waved his hand at the fireplace and the flames grew higher, easing the tension in my shaking muscles.

"How do you do that?"

"It's part of what I am."

"And what are you?"

He just stared into the fireplace.

"Okay, if you won't say what *you* are, will you at least tell me what that *thing* was?"

He nodded. This seemed safer territory to him. "It was a construct, a creature made from clay by an individual in the far future whose name is Kanor. Let's just say he does not have kind wishes towards humanity."

"Why was it pretending to be my mum?"

His head made a wobbling gesture of uncertainty. "I'm not entirely sure. I do know that you are destined to be a threat to Kanor. My guess is that your so-called parents were sort of prison guards."

"Why didn't this Kanor just kill me?"

"Again, uncertain."

I sighed and stretched my legs out in front of the soothing heat. "How many of those construct things have you come across before?"

"None. This was the first time that I'd seen one in the flesh."

I looked up at my nameless lodger. He was staring deep into the fire. "So, where did you learn how to kill it?"

"I haven't the foggiest idea," he replied, "and that seriously bothers me."

We sat for a while in silence with only the crackling of the fire and the creaking of the chair cutting across the stillness of the room. Eventually, I asked him, "Who were the woman and the girl in my dream?"

My erstwhile lodger smiled warmly. "The girl was your sister. Your twin, in fact."

"Oh."

He nodded.

"What's her name?"

"I don't know. Sorry."

"Where is she?"

"Again, I don't know."

I nodded. "The woman… I said she was our mother."

He gave another quiet nod. "Eloise." The name was not more than a breath and I could swear that there was a flare of light behind his dark glasses for just an instant.

"You know her, don't you?"

"Very well."

"How?"

He seemed to consider his reply very carefully. "We come from the same place."

"Which is?"

"So many damned questions," he grumbled, idly tossing a small flame from his finger towards the fire.

"Are you surprised?"

His lips turned up in a begrudging smile. "I guess not." He leaned against the edge of the stone fireplace, his eyes studying me from behind his dark glasses. A curious smile touched his lips.

"What?"

"It's just weird," he shrugged, "seeing you here. In the flesh."

"What do you mean?"

He held his hand out to the fire and a small flame jumped up to his fingertips. Twisting and twirling his fingers, he manipulated the flame as if it were a trickster's coin, dancing across the back of his knuckles. "Where I come from, I saw lots of things. Some of them were godawful. Terrifying, brutal, despairing. Others… Others were strangely reassuring, comforting." He pointed to me, the flame dancing on his fingertip. "You were one of the latter. You and your sister. Whenever I watched the pair of you, I felt a warmth, a satisfaction, that I could not explain."

"You do realise how creepy that sounds?"

He chuckled and closed his hand, snuffing out the little flame. "I know. Like I said…"

"Complicated."

"It's why I chose to come and hide in you. Things went sour, accusations were made. I had to lie low somewhere that others couldn't find me. You were ideal."

"Should I be flattered?"

Child of Light

He shrugged. "I think it's more a case that I should be grateful. It can't have been easy for you, especially as your *powers* started to develop."

I thought back to fighting the construct and shuddered.

"So, what now?"

He seemed to ponder this a moment before saying, "How about we stop the obliteration of everything?"

I looked up at the weird individual that had turned my dull life upside down, let out a sharp puff of air and said, "Sure. Why not?"

I was standing before two doors: one white, one black.

Now, this in itself may not seem that odd, but the fact that they were the only things to be seen for miles around, made it feel all the more surreal. It was a grassy hillside in the middle of nowhere and, not only that, we hadn't exactly walked there. He (still didn't know his name) had told me to lie down on the bed in the cabin and close my eyes. With a certain amount of mistrust, I had done as he had asked and had felt a warm fingertip touch me between my eyes. The darkness behind my eyelids had dissolved and was replaced with the current view.

"Where are we?"

He cocked his head to one side and frowned. "Somewhere and nowhere," he explained in a cryptic fashion. "Technically, you're still on that little bed in a shack in the arse-end of Scotland, but your consciousness is going on a small voyage — an educational trip, one might say. Just like that one you went on to the castle when you were seven."

I nodded. "But with crazy doors instead of some old

paedo dressed up as Oliver Cromwell."

He grinned. "That's the idea!" He gestured to the doors: "These represent two possible futures for creation."

I looked over the two plain doors that were just the same as you would find in any non-supernatural, modern-day house that had been decked out by a builder with a healthy credit account at the local Wickes. "Let me guess: one good, one bad?"

He nodded. "Some time back, before I had to run off with my proverbial tail between my legs, I saw a wondrous thing. Heaven and the Physical Realm were to be united. God came down to Earth, on His living throne, all the angels singing His divine glory. The two Realms would combine, forming an eternal paradise where humans walked with angels in the presence of God. This event," he pointed to the white door, "was the Convergence."

The palm of my right hand suddenly felt slick with sweat and my fingers twitched. My teeth chewed at my lips.

"Go on," he said, "Open it."

I turned the golden knob and the door swung open. A bright white light engulfed me and I was aware of voices. So many voices. They were talking, laughing, singing, praising. The joy was indescribable. My jaw dropped, my eyes closed and tears streamed down my cheeks. I felt it calling out to me, drawing me in, and I placed one foot towards the door. A firm but not unkind hand fell on my shoulder and the doorknob was removed from my grasp as the door was closed.

I blinked and turned to face my companion. My mouth moved but no words came. Nothing could adequately describe my emotions.

He just nodded.

As one, we faced the second door. I swallowed and reached out to the pewter doorknob. As I grasped the dull metal, I felt the pit of my stomach roll over. Turning the handle caused the door to swing open and I saw...

Nothing.

On the other side of the portal, there was blackness. But it wasn't like the blackness of the night sky up to which you might gaze, filled with awe at what might be out there beyond your vision. As I gazed into this obsidian void, there was the firm knowledge that nothing existed there: no galaxies, no worlds, no creatures, not even the smallest particle or atom.

There was absolutely nothing.

"What... what caused this?"

"Not a *what*. A *who*." My erstwhile lodger stood by my shoulder and stared alongside me into the nothing. "Sometime soon, an individual will arise and set things in motion that will lead to this. Rather than a *Con*vergence, there will be a *Di*vergence. Heaven and Earth will never become one. Humans will never know the paradise that was promised to them. Instead, constructs will stalk the planet, decimating humanity, reducing them to a pitiful remnant to serve their overlord: Kanor. Then, after all the horror and bloodshed, everything will be swept away, obliterated."

"Can it be stopped?"

"I sincerely hope so."

"How?"

"Right now, I don't know. But, to start with, we need to fill in a certain amount of blanks that we both seem to possess." He flicked his wrist and the door slammed shut.

"Fortunately, I know someone who might be able to help us."

Then he clicked his fingers and everything was white.

"Where are we?"

"Somewhere very special to me," my companion said, his head turning left and right as if he was making sure we could not be seen, even though wherever we were seemed decidedly empty. "But, more on that in a moment. First, I need you to do something for me."

I frowned. "What?"

"The beings from this place mustn't know that we're here." He waved a hand to dismiss my concerned frown. "It's not like that. I *will* explain, but we have to make sure they can't see us. It would cause too many complications. You can make us appear invisible."

"Really…?"

He nodded. "Think back to when you were at school, when you were daydreaming. No one noticed, did they? You did it then, just without realising. You unconsciously created an illusion around yourself that you weren't really there. You can do that here, right now. Just imagine the pair of us in a huge, shiny bubble that lets light pass all the way through, showing the casual observer what's on the other side of us. That way the inhabitants here won't see us. As long as we're quiet about it, that is."

I frowned. It sounded somewhat far-fetched, but what the hell… I did as I was asked and visualised a shining bubble around us. Its surface glistened in the whiteness and, as far as I could tell, it masked our presence. "Done," I said. "How will we know if it works?"

Child of Light

I realised, in shock, that we were about to find out as two angels walked into view out of the whiteness. I made to state the obvious, but my companion held up a finger to silence me, so I sealed my lips around the unsaid comment. The two winged beings walked towards us, deep in conversation. As they talked, I listened, and it was the most bizarre conversation I had ever heard. Not so much due to the content; they were talking about God and Heaven (which I was sort of guessing was where we were) and other deep philosophical concepts which, quite frankly, were far beyond me. It was *how* they were talking which was odd. The language that they spoke was definitely not anything that I had ever heard on Earth. It was sonorous and complex, consonants dancing with vowels as they pirouetted off the beings' tongues. However, I was able to understand every single word as they walked past us without so much as a second glance.

My companion smiled. "Well done! Now let's get going. As we walk, I'll give you angelology 101." So, he did. He told me that the two angels we had seen were Angeloi, the lowest level and most common type. Above them were the four Archangels who were allowed in the Tabernacle, to minister to the Presence of God. Then there were the Dominions, small angels that were rarely seen around Heaven, and Powers, hermetic entities that remained secluded in their own part of the realm. "Thrones," he continued, "speak for themselves. They're angels that make up the Throne of the Presence." He smiled. "They're cute little things. You know that funny toy you had that chatted a lot when you were little?"

"My Furby?"

"Yep. Just like that." He paused.

"What is it?"

"Then there's one more angel. He holds the rank of Seraphim — the most powerful of them all. He actually dwelt in the heart of the Presence. This was his reward for helping to initiate Creation right back at the beginning of known time. His song resonated through the void and pleased God so much that the Deity took the melody and made it manifest.

"Whilst in the Presence, he was privileged to view the timeline. He saw many things. Many good; many bad. He saw that Heaven and the Physical Realm were to combine, the hellish realm known as Beyond, being obliterated in the process, and he rejoiced at this. But then he saw a confusing darkness fall across the timeline and it split apart, it diverged. Heaven never converged with Earth and Kanor rose, his monsters destroying all that was good. Then, finally, there was nothing, oblivion.

"The seraph knew that he had to do something. He tried to speak out, but he was betrayed and he had to flee this place. He had to hide somewhere that he had seen in the timeline. Somewhere safe."

My voice cracked as I asked the obvious question, "What was the seraph's name?"

He reached up and removed his glasses. Two fiery orbs watched for my reaction as he said, "I am Lucifer. I am the Light that came before all Creation. I dwelt in the Heart of God and my song of worship forged the Realms. I mean you no harm."

I stared at those fiery eyes and focused on what lay behind them, as I had done with the construct. Whereas, with the clay monster, there had been a void, here there was so much life, vitality and, above all, passion. This being, this seraph, was the most alive person I had ever met. And I felt no malice in him toward me at all.

I nodded.

Lucifer replaced his dark glasses. "We're here," he said as we entered a space that contained a golden throne atop a small dais. In front of the seat was a small platform. The seraph walked over to this, knelt down and ran his hand across the surface. He shuddered and stood up.

"What's wrong?"

"A memory. I think." He shook his head. "There's so much that I can't remember."

"And you would like to know, Light, wouldn't you?"

The voice was female and incredibly melodious. As the tuneful words reached my ears, I felt a threefold rhythm waltz across the synapses of my brain. As one, Lucifer and I turned to face its source, a girl about my age who was definitely not human. Her hair was grey and flowed down past her shoulders, over a long dress that seemed to shimmer with what looked to me like fireflies. Her eyes were pure water and where she passed remained wet for a while before the moisture evaporated.

"I have been expecting you. It has been such a long time for you, but a blink of an eye for me."

With that, the girl was gone and a middle-aged woman took her place. The hair and the clothing were the same, but the voice had changed, subtly ageing and somewhat deeper in timbre.

"How can she see us?" I asked the seraph. "I've still got my mojo turned up."

Lucifer cocked his head to one side as he considered my question before he smiled knowingly. "The Abyss sees just about everything. She is a living sea that encompasses the three Realms, encircling Time and Space."

The woman walked over to me, her form now shifting to that of an old woman, her voice matching her looks. "More or less everything that has been, is and will be is within my knowledge Twin," her cracked words stated enigmatically. "Almost nothing can remain hidden from the waters of Time." She turned to face my companion. "Which is why you're here."

He nodded. "We both need answers, the boy and I."

"But," replied the girl as she cocked her head, "What is the question?"

"What is it that perplexes you the most?" the woman asked.

"What is it you haven't told the Twin?" the crone smiled, a glint in her eye. "What is it that you suspect, but dare not wish for? That is clouded by your past and future."

The three-in-one reached out a hand and the air in front of us became a dense mist of water vapour, in which figures started to form. I watched as my real mother came into view. Her hands rested on her swollen stomach and her lips moved silently in unheard conversation. Her face showed concern as another figure emerged from the mist.

A familiar figure.

The one standing next to me.

I heard Lucifer's breath catch as he saw this other version of himself. "Is this what *could* happen or what *will* happen?" he asked, his voice low and barely audible.

"All we show you…" began the girl.

"…is the truth," finished the woman.

"How you interpret it, is up to you," stated the crone.

Eloise was talking frantically to Lucifer, every now

Child of Light

and then looking over her shoulder as if a distance noise was causing a distraction. They were standing in a courtyard, a grand fountain in the shape of a serpent behind them, its waters cascading down onto dusty mud brick. Eloise grabbed Lucifer's arm and pulled at him, seeming to beg him to follow her into a large building off to the side, but the seraph resolutely shook his head and replied something that we could not hear. He reached out, cupped my mother's cheek in his hand and gently pulled her face to his before kissing her warmly on the lips. When they parted, the shared love on their faces was unmistakable. Lucifer smiled, knelt down on the dusty floor and leaned the side of his face against her stomach before pulling back and whispering something to the babies within. Then, standing up, he pulled over his head an animalistic mask that bore a pair of imposing antlers, turned and walked away.

Eloise placed her face in her hands and wept.

The image faded.

Lucifer and I stood in silence. We turned our heads and mutely stared at each other.

"This is why you were drawn to the boy," explained the girl.

The seraph rounded on the entity as it morphed once again into the shape of the woman. "I have no memory of this. When is it?"

"What does your heart tell you?" asked the woman.

"That's time travel's a bitch," the seraph spat. "Where is his sister? Where is my daughter?"

"That is not for you to know right now," the crone said, before firmly sealing her withered lips in a tight line.

"Like hell, it's not!" Lucifer roared, his hands erupting into flame. "You will tell me where my other child is!"

"Watch your tone, Light," the girl frowned.

"We are not to be challenged," the woman growled.

"There are far more pressing matters at hand," the crone explained.

I watched as Lucifer forced himself to swallow down his anger and the flames on his fists died out. "The Divergence," he nodded. "What will cause it? How can it be stopped?"

The girl replaced the crone. "How can one prevent something that has already happened?"

"It may have already occurred to you, but not to us."

"Can you be so sure of that, Light?" asked the woman. "Can you be so sure of anything?"

Lucifer seemed to ponder this. "I need to know what has happened. Everything is so…" he waved his hand around his head, "clouded. I can't fully comprehend everything that has or will happen to me. I keep seeing glimpses of a life I can't possibly have lived. That which you showed us, for example. That was in the Indus Valley, wasn't it? Yet, I have no memory of it whatsoever. Has it already happened? Is part of my memory missing? Or will it occur in the future? Please, send us back there. Let us see what happened there. Once my memory is clear, I will be able to put things right."

"And do what?" asked the girl.

"Stop the Divergence."

The middle-aged woman shook her head and said, "Now why…"

"…would you want to do that?" finished the crone.

Lucifer opened his mouth to reply but, before he could speak, the girl, the woman and the crone stood before us together, held out their hands and we were no longer in Heaven.

Chapter Three

There were two things that immediately struck me: it was very dark and it was very warm. I cast my eyes upwards and observed a normal night sky above me. Orion rose into the black, wielding his club in his usual threatening manner as he strode across the battlefield of the cosmos. Looking left and right, I saw what seemed to be small dwellings made from brown-coloured bricks. I took a step towards one and felt the ground crunch underfoot. Pausing, I glanced down and saw sand scattered along the narrow road.

That was odd. Lucifer had said that my vision of my non-past had been in the Indus Valley. As far as I was aware, that area was not known for sand in the streets.

I resumed my inspection of the house in front of me. Running my fingers over the bricks, they felt dry and baked. Were they clay? Something inside of me shuddered at that word. I looked up at the lintel over the doorway and frowned. It had been marked with a substance that appeared both black and shiny in the vague light of nighttime. I reached up and touched the dark smear and grimaced as my fingertips came away sticky.

It was as I bent down to wipe my fingers clean in the dusty sand that the screams started to rise up from all around me.

It was also then that I realised I was completely alone. Lucifer was nowhere to be seen.

So, first things first: self-preservation. I repeated what the seraph had told me to do in Heaven. I visualised a large protective bubble around myself.

Next: noise. If I thought that the volume of the buzzing in my head had been bad back home, its level here was absolutely intolerable! As a horde of wasps careened around inside my head, I slumped down onto my haunches with my back propped against a wall to prevent me from falling over. My hands shot to my ears in a futile attempt to block out the overwhelming sound. Wherever I had been sent was obviously far busier than my home town or school. It was as if thousands of people were screaming inside my brain. I closed my eyes and felt warm tears trickle down my cheeks before I shook my head in frustration. I couldn't let this overwhelm me. I was somewhere strange and possibly hostile. I needed my wits about me. I thought back to how I had defeated the construct in the kitchen by mentally seeing what I took to be its brain. I envisaged the buzzing noise as a swarming black mass, like a depression cloud above a cartoon character, then I took a blue blanket and threw it over the raging ball of scribbles, pulling the material down tight. It undulated and struggled in my grip but I successfully tied a mental knot at its base and the reverberating drone fell to a muffled hum. Sighing, I opened my eyes and nodded to myself. It was good to learn new skills.

Finally: investigation. There was no point just sitting cowering in a corner. I needed to find out exactly

Child of Light

where the Abyss had sent me and what had happened to my travelling companion. So, albeit rather cautiously, I headed off down the road on which I had seemingly appeared out of nowhere.

It didn't take me long to stumble across signs of life. I turned around a corner and emerged into a small square. In its middle stood a reasonably sized statue. It was of a severe-looking, bare-chested man who was seated upon a throne. Around his neck was an ornate necklace that was adorned with a spherical gem. Whereas the statue was predominantly the natural colour of the stonework, the round ornament had been painted bright green. I stood, staring up at the likeness, and decided that this was definitely someone that I would not want to cross. There was such arrogance in his eyes. They spoke of someone who would kill first and ask questions later rather than listen to explanations of failure.

I became aware of noises from the other side of the square and saw a group of seven or eight men enter. They were dressed in what appeared to be simple homespun clothing and their skin looked somewhat swarthy in colour, their hair dark. They carried ropes and an assortment of what appeared to be tools. Not noticing me at all (which was a relief), they headed over to the statue and began to shout at it in a harsh tongue I couldn't understand, but their violent gesturing left little to the imagination. After a few minutes of verbal abuse, they slung their ropes up around the statue's head and began to heave. It didn't take long for the statue to begin to rock. As it did, the group of men became more excited and their shouts started to increase in volume, leading them to pull even harder. After a couple more attempts, the statue crashed forward onto the ground. It cracked into three large chunks: its base, its torso, and its head. The head rolled listlessly across the floor of the square until it came to rest on its side, glaring at its attackers who whooped for joy, gathered up their tools and headed off down a side alley, presumably to look for more statuary to desecrate.

After wondering for a brief moment what the subject of the monument had done to incur such treatment, I too headed off in search of more answers.

I wandered around a city in turmoil. On the face of it, I seemed to have landed in the middle of some sort of revolution. Time and time again I either encountered groups of citizens destroying statues of the arrogant-looking man adorned with the green stone, or evidence of their work. Statuary lay smashed, murals were daubed with paint, carvings had been chipped away. Whoever he was, they really did not like him.

However, there was something else in the air that night. Something far darker.

I kept having the distinct feeling that I was not alone in my wanderings through the city. Every now and then, it was as if a breeze had passed me and the presence of some other being had brushed against mine. Then, shortly after this occurrence, a dreadful scream would rise up into the night, as if someone had lost something most dear to them.

After the seventh time that this had happened, I began to wonder if it was the reason that I was there, my logic being that two odd things in one place at the same time seemed to be more than just a coincidence. Staying inside my *safety bubble*, I reached out with my mind and began to study all those around me. There was a cacophony of emotions: ecstatic jubilation; a great sense of loss; devout calm; something entirely different.

I focussed on this last one. It felt like it was dotted around the city and belonged to individuals rather than some sort of entity. Something about it made the hairs on the back of my neck stand to attention.

Whatever was causing this emotion wasn't human. It was a cold, efficient feeling about a job that needed to be done quickly and without hesitation.

As I stood there, reaching out, I felt one pocket of this emotion draw to a stop in a nearby alleyway. I ran as fast as I could to find out what its source was. The sight that greeted me is one that I will never forget. By the doorway to a small house stood a figure adorned in loose black clothing. At its feet were the limp bodies of two adults — a quick scan of their minds told me they were just unconscious. In the being's arms was a small child that looked about four or five. The infant was screaming for all it was worth as the dark being had sunk its teeth into the child's neck. I watched paralysed as the child grew quieter and quieter until it lay still in the feasting creature's arms.

But that was not the end of it.

The creature in black continued to drink until the child was just dust. The desiccated particles drifted down from its arms to join the sand on the floor.

I could not help but shout out.

That may have been a mistake.

My mojo must have dipped, as the creature's face snapped up and their eyes latched upon me. I could see then that it was female.

And it was quick.

There was a blur of motion and her hands were on my shoulders, her nose up close to my skin as she appeared to inhale. She pulled back and gasped then barked something at me in a language I did not understand.

My mouth flapped open and shut in terror.

She repeated the same thing again.

"I... I don't understand."

The being frowned and took a step back, her hands still holding my shoulders but not as tight. She gave a small nod, then muttered something that seemed less severe.

"Okay," I said in my most quiet and non-threatening manner, "I'm going to try something. Please don't freak out and kill me."

The creature frowned and then gasped as I sank down inside her head. Images flooded over me. There were pictures of her as a child, a human child with parents and siblings. Then, when she was older, she became sick. Someone came to her hut and bent over her, a warm liquid flowed into her mouth and she fell asleep. When she awoke she was reborn as something newer and stronger. I swallowed. *She was a vampire*. Here in front of me was an honest-to-God, walking and talking creature out of the horror books. Not only that, but she had a mission. Her saviour had told her three things that she should follow and I felt their meaning, rather than hear them in her native tongue: *Find the Eternals; Protect the Twins; Await the Divergence*. So she had done as she had been told. Over long years, she had joined with others of her kind in hunting down constructs. Wherever those golems lurked, her kind was there to eradicate them.

She had arrived at this city because its last king had infested the place with the mindless killing machines. He had been overthrown by the new ruler but, as an act of vengeance, he had done something so abominable, so vilo, that I felt myself begin to cry. He had taken all the firstborns of the city into his palace and slaughtered them, replacing them with constructs that looked just like them. He had then sent them home to their unsuspecting families. Every single family in the settlement had a sleeper agent waiting to be activated to slaughter them when this callous ex-ruler saw fit. All the families, that was, except the community of foreigners that kept themselves to themselves. They had disobeyed the ruler and not sent their children to the palace on that fateful day. So, in order to show that there was no construct in their house, they had smeared lambs' blood on their lintels.

The vampires had descended that night in order to eradicate the construct threat. They were to destroy all the firstborns of the city except for those of the houses daubed with blood — a bloody Passover, but not as it appeared in the Bible. As I continued to rifle through her subconscious, I saw an image of their leader, a figure that chilled me to the core. He looked like an angel, but he wore long dark robes and his wings were burnt, bent and black. In his hand, he carried a sword that seemed to sing to the night sky. He stalked through the city like Death, looking for all that he could slay. He was Destruction.

And then the woman's thoughts abruptly ceased as she screamed out in agony.

And so did I.

It was a pain that I had never felt before, so excruciating that my mind was boggled as to how I was still standing. I looked down at a face that knew it was dying. Protruding from the vampire's chest was a small lance covered in blood. This same lance had also impaled me. We were joined together like a type of grisly kebab.

The weapon drew back through her body and she fell limp in my hands. I looked up and saw, standing behind her, a child of about five. But it was definitely not human. Its right arm was long and extended into the shape of a lance. It stared at me, the same puzzlement that I was experiencing as to why I was not dead clearly apparent in its eyes. Not for an instant taking my eyes off the child-shaped construct, I winced as I ran my fingers over my damp chest. They came away scarlet.

The construct decided that it was time to back away.

I glowered and it froze in its tracks, unable to move. As I bore down on its mind, it started to squeal. Its lance changed shape and became a serrated saw which turned upon its owner. Once again, remembering my confrontation back home, I smiled in grim satisfaction as I had it drag the blade through its own body. But this time there was no fire-wielding seraph to finish the job, so I had to ensure that the construct stayed dead. As the serrated blade sawed itself down the middle, I envisioned the clay from which it was made returning to the earth from where it had come. Its squeal became a horrific collection of gurgles as its body liquified and drained away into the ground. A more final result compared to my previous construct-slaying. It would appear that I was now definitely learning on the job.

Swallowing hard, I unzipped my hoodie and pulled up my blood-stained t-shirt to examine my wound. I wiped my fingers through the blood on my skin but found no gaping hole. There just appeared to be a thin white line where the lance had punctured me. The pain was also abating.

Well, that was useful, if somewhat disturbing.

Child of Light

I glanced around and saw a knife sheathed in the belt of the dead vampire. I picked it up and dragged the blade across the back of my hand then watched in fascination as the wound bound back up. My mind started to race. Was this new? Had I always healed fast? I thought back to times I had fallen over as a youngster, my father running over with a clean handkerchief which he wiped over the cut or graze and proclaiming, "Good as new, Champ!" What would he have done had I broken a leg?

I didn't have any more time to wonder as something heavy struck me at the base of my skull and everything turned black.

When I came to, I was aware of two immediate sensations. First, the back of my head was pounding. Second, someone was slapping me harshly across my face. Neither of these was in any way agreeable.

I groaned and began to open my eyes. The hushed sound of someone muttering something in an unintelligible language limped its way into my ears. I strained to hear what they were saying, but the discomfort of my aching head refused to cooperate with my auditory sense.

"Where…?" was all I was able to manage before my head started to scream once more.

At least the slapping had stopped.

A second voice joined the first. From its inflection, I guessed it was asking a question. Ignoring the screaming from the base of my skull, I cranked my eyelids open the rest of the way and was rewarded with the sight of two dark-clad individuals peering down at me in a less than kindly fashion. Their black robes were identical — plain and utilitarian, just like the vampire I had seen in the alley. One was male, the other female. Both were apparently very confused.

It was dark, so still nighttime then, but I was able to make out that I was now inside, away from the carnage of a city in chaos. Opposite me, down the far end of the room, stood a statue of the man with the green stone. This had been daubed with paint, but even through the red smear, the man managed to scowl a feeling of righteous imperialism.

My attention was drawn back to my two captors as the female, a slightly built redhead, snapped something at her compatriot who, in response, just shrugged. The redhead rolled her green eyes and then turned back to their prisoner, barking out a question.

All I could manage right then was a vague shrug.

Her green eyes narrowed and she crossed her arms. Another question came, then a third. I frowned. Each one was asked in what felt like a different language. I just shook my head. This was not the response that Red had wanted and she grunted in dissatisfaction before turning to her less vocal companion and snapping something at him. The poor man held up his hands in protest and backed off, pointing at me and shaking his head violently.

My gut had the feeling that this wasn't good. Not good at all.

This instinct was confirmed when Red's hand snatched out faster than I could perceive and grasped my jaw in her vice-like fingers. I felt myself being dragged to my rather unsteady feet and her face was now directly in front of me. Her lips drew back, revealing two deadly sharp fangs.

I swallowed and willed myself not to vomit in terror.

I tried to calm myself, to reach out and touch the

vampire's consciousness, but my own mind was racing, galloping through varying fields of crazy and I just couldn't focus.

Red drew her head back to bite down when a shout came from the back of the room. I found myself being thrown roughly to the stone floor. I swore loudly as I landed on my shoulder. I swore even louder as a swift kick from Red's foot caught me in the stomach before she and her companion stalked off out of the room.

Grunting and groaning, I heaved myself into a sitting position and became aware of a figure at the far end of the room, just out of sight in the deep shadows. It spoke in the same language that I had heard the angels use in Heaven.

"What are you?"

"Confused. Hurting. Tired. Choose one," I snapped back.

"Also apparently English," came a British tongue. "Well, isn't that intriguing?" There was a soft movement and an anthropomorphic shadow broke free of the gloom. I kind of wished it hadn't. There, walking over to me was something that looked far worse than a vampire. It was their leader, the one that I had seen in the vampire's mind before the construct had killed her. He was male, tall and broad, clad in long, black flowing robes that rustled as he walked cautiously across the room. Behind him were two large black, bent and burnt wings. His face was deathly white with pronounced shadows around the cheeks and under the eyes — eyes that were aflame. These burning eyes drew level with me as the creature knelt down on one knee in order to study my face and my clothing. His brow knotted and he murmured, "I know you."

I shook my head, ignoring the discomfort. "Trust

me, I think I would remember if I'd had the dubious pleasure."

The corner of the being's lips turned up just a fraction and it actually chuckled. "I didn't look like…" he ran long, slender fingers down his sallow cheek, "…this. It was at All Saints. The day the crucifix cried and the *Kidsweek* concert was cancelled. You were with the paranormal investigator. Spallucci."

I grimaced. "Sorry. Still no clue." I paused. "I was at home with my…" I thought about the creatures that had been my captors. "I was at home for *Kidsweek*. Saw it all on the telly. And I certainly don't know a church called All Saints."

The being's head cocked thoughtfully to one side in a manner that struck me as vaguely familiar. "Perhaps I'm thinking of the wrong one."

"Yeah. Definitely not me."

"No." The being shook his head. "That's not what I meant. Definitely you. Perhaps wrong *Kidsweek*. Who the hell are you?"

"Like I said, just someone who's confused, hurting and tired. Tell you what, we could trade."

The being raised an eyebrow in question.

"I'll tell you mine if you tell me yours."

"That could be problematic."

"My life seems to be full of problems at the moment. What's one more?"

My captor remained resolutely silent.

I shrugged. "Okay, let's try a different one." I pointed to the defaced statue. "Where am I?"

"Egypt, in its infancy."

I nodded. I should really have guessed that from the sand that was underfoot everywhere and the accompanying bloody Passover. "Second, who's Ozymandias over there?"

The pale-faced being snatched a glance over his shoulder and, when his face returned to me, there was overwhelming hatred in his eyes. "That," he snarled, "would be my brother."

"I'm guessing there's some sibling rivalry then? He responsible for your makeover?"

"Asmodeus took everything from me. It was he who saw to it that I was cast out of Heaven. I fell for aeons in the fiery waters that surround the three Realms."

I swallowed. "The Abyss."

His eyes narrowed. "You're not just a boy, are you." It was a definite statement rather than a question. "What are you?" He reached out and his cold hand cupped my cheek. As it did so…

…I was standing apart from everything. There was nothing beneath me aside from space. Dark, infinite space. And *that* was burning. All around me, a song echoed through the fiery firmament, a three-fold rhythm that caused every bone in my minuscule body to vibrate, to resonate with a tune older than time itself.

We are one.
We are one.
We are one.

I gasped and felt the insides of my lungs scorch as I saw what rose into the darkness before me. It was a being larger than any planet. Consisting purely of incandescent flame, six enormous wings spread out behind it and, in its outstretched arms, it grasped a sword and a chalice. The Titan's lips were moving in time to the threefold tune as it swung the sword, piercing the very fabric of reality.

Out of the wound in space-time, waters began to

pour. The song increased in intensity as the waters swirled around all that was, had been and would now never be. They clung to every single atom, every quark, every discernible particle and dragged them down, down, down into the bowl of the chalice which gobbled up all that existed with an insatiable hunger.

Then finally, the waters, the living waters that surrounded everything, rejoiced at the completion of their work and they too dove into the cup, singing exultantly as they did so.

And there was nothing.

I snapped back to the here and now, or the there and then perhaps to be more precise, and was confronted with a look of shock on the being's face. Had he witnessed the same vision or had he seen something different?

Was the apocalyptic Titan I had seen in my vision this being right here in front of me? Would he be the destruction of everything?

I instinctively knew the answer.

I also knew that I had to escape.

Opportunity presented itself in the form of Red charging back into the room, shouting something in her unintelligible tongue. The pale-faced being turned to see what the commotion was and, in that instant, I flashed my safety bubble around myself and began to run. I pounded my way out of the door, past the red-headed vampire and didn't dare to look back.

It is a very surreal feeling to walk through a precise moment in history. I think, when we read about certain events in books or watch programmes about them on the telly, we form images of them or our own little movie scenes that portray them in our heads. The Normandy landings: allied forces running up beaches with German troops shooting down every alternate soldier. The Battle of Hastings: absolute carnage in a field in southeast England until one single arrow stops it all.

For me, I guess like most people, the Passover and the final plague of Egypt, the Death of the Firstborn, was, well… very Biblical. I'd always imagined it as something quietly taking place in the dead of night when everyone was asleep, a mysterious force drifting through a sleeping city, silently snuffing out the lives of all the firstborn young. I certainly did not have an image of a city in open rebellion whilst an organised cadre of vampires stalked the streets draining the life force from clay cuckoos that had replaced the real firstborns who had been brutally murdered sometime before.

I guess we never really know exactly what happens in history, especially the further away it is from our current point in time.

As I wandered blindly through those Ancient Egyptian streets that brutal night, part of me was actually fascinated by the whole thing and wanted to stop and watch the proceedings. I guess that was perfectly natural. I mean, how often does one really have the chance to participate in a momentous event in history? However, I was also aware that I did not want to get stuck in the past, no matter how interesting it might be. So I carried on looking for Lucifer as, all around me, a city screamed.

As it happened, I found someone else.

Down some sort of side street off a random square in God knew where in the city, a girl in her late teens or early twenties sat with her back to a mud-brick wall. She held her head in her hands, her fingers clenching her blonde hair that was streaked with red. Curiously, she seemed to be wearing a white nightdress over which appeared to be draped a dirt-encrusted makeshift shawl.

I carefully approached her, ensuring that my safety bubble was still intact. With every footstep, my heart began to beat louder. Then, when I was just a couple of metres away, she dropped her hands into her lap, sat up straight, turned her face towards me and frowned.

I swallowed as I looked into the face of my mother. My mother who, apparently, could see me.

Her crystal blue eyes never left my face as she pulled herself unsteadily to her feet, her hands using the wall as a support. They scanned my face and then noted the bloodstain on my shirt. "You're hurt," she said in a well-spoken British accent.

"It's okay," I shrugged. "It healed."

She nodded, apparently accepting the fact that what had obviously been a fatal wound had become no more than a scratch. "I know you. From All Saints. You were there. With the investigator."

A small smile touched my lips. "So I've already been informed. I don't think that's happened for me yet. Time travel's a bitch."

Her lips curled up in an imitation of mine and she came closer, her eyes continuing to study my face. "Your eyes. They're so familiar." She shook her head. "Sorry, I guess that sounds weird. I'm just confused. I ended up here and I'm looking for someone, but I can't find him."

"Looks like we're in the same boat. You go first. Who's your missing person?"

"That's the thing," she sighed. "I'm not so sure now. So much has changed. He was my age, at least he *ap-*

peared to be. Then, there was this fight. Not between us; between him and this other person. An incredibly powerful being. Well, he became what he really is: a fallen angel, would you believe?" She shook her head in her own disbelief at her situation. "I mean, he's got the whole vibe going on. Black robes, pale skin, fiery eyes, black burnt wings…" She paused as I frowned. "Have you seen him?"

I nodded. "Our paths crossed just before." The emotions emanating from my mother were impossible to miss, even for someone without my apparent talents. Emotions which certainly conflicted with the image that the Abyss had shown me of her in a loving relationship with Lucifer. "You love him very much, don't you?"

She nodded. "I'm just afraid that he's doing something terrible."

I recalled the images from the dead vampire's mind. "May I ask, what's his name?"

"Well, I used to know him as James, but that was a very long time ago. His actual name is Abaddon." A tear edged its way out of her eye and trickled down her cheek.

I reached out instinctively to brush the tear away and, as I did, my finger touched her warm skin and, in that moment, I knew something incredible. Deep inside my mother, something was growing. No, not one thing: *two* things. They were still multiplying at exponential rates on the cellular level, but in her womb, the seeds were sown for me and my sister. Two sets of DNA were tangoing together, pirouetting their way into new life. Eloise's DNA and…

I flinched and took a step backwards, my eyes wide open.

Eloise gasped, a mixture of wonder and confusion on her face. Her hands dropped to her middle and they ran over her nightdress. She looked back up at me, her face radiating a warm smile which suddenly evaporated as she glanced over my shoulder.

I was aware of the sound of heavy footsteps behind me and a hand gently fell on my shoulder as I became aware of a familiar presence.

"Alec?"

I heard the question in Lucifer's voice, but I was more concentrated on the terror that now filled my mother's eyes. Her head was shaking from side to side and she began to back away from us, her hand pressed against the wall to stop her from collapsing in dread. There was the impression of movement behind her and a figure emerged from the gloom. Even before the white moonlight revealed the familiar pale features of the being to whom the vampires had taken me, I knew exactly who it was. I had felt part of him just before, his DNA performing the age-old dance with that of my mother. So, as the pale face of Abaddon glared at the being behind me, I knew that the fallen angel and possible destroyer of reality had to be my father.

The image of an affectionate Lucifer talking to the babies in Eloise's womb resurfaced in my confused mind and I shook my head.

The seraph's grip on my shoulder tightened. "I can feel the Abyss pulling us away. It's time to go," he whispered.

And everything around us faded away.

Chapter Four

I did what any sane, rational being would do upon discovering that their father was a fallen angel destined to bring about the end of everything.

I threw up.

My hands gripped the slender trunk of some sort of tree and the contents of my stomach emptied out onto the floor of wherever it was that Lucifer and I had been transported to. As my stomach started to stop heaving, I became aware of the strong smell of roasted tobacco. I turned my head just a fraction to observe my travelling companion leaning against another tree. He was drawing on one of his cigarettes, thoughtfully gazing at the smoke that its flaming tip produced.

"Where did you actually get those?"

He took another long draw and regarded the battered, crumpled pack. "They're Lucky Strikes," the seraph observed. "I feel like I should know where I originally got them from, but it's dancing just out of the reach of my memory." He blew a smoke ring into the air. "Just like so many things. You want one?"

I shook my head, then regretted the movement.

"Use your power. Convince yourself that you're not nauseous."

I frowned. "You think that's possible?"

"Don't know unless you try."

In my mind, I saw myself drinking a long relaxing cup of warm ginger cordial, its soothing properties quelling the acids in my stomach. I drew myself up, let out a long breath and looked around. Two things immediately struck me: it was now daytime; we were no longer in Egypt but somewhere not too far away. The environment had a similar ambience: it was warm, the landscape was still somewhat arid and the flora seemed to suggest somewhere close to the Mediterranean. As for the time period, there didn't appear to be any trappings of the twenty-first century. There were no pylons, no telephone masts, no wind turbines and no drone of a nearby motorway. Instead, there was a dirt road and a bored-looking guy bouncing along in a cart that was being pulled by a just as bored-looking ox. Neither human nor ox paid us any attention as they and their cargo headed along the road to what appeared to present itself as a nearby city.

Lucifer pulled away from the tree and allowed his eyes to wander down the road toward the small city. It sat atop a hill overlooking a valley that curved around its base. Tall, threatening walls seemed to enclose everything. There appeared to be no movement in the countryside around and about.

The seraph looked at me. With a shrug, he suggested we follow the cart, and we headed off along the road.

"Where did you get to?" I asked as we walked along the rutted track.

"The middle of the carnage. Did *you* see much?"

I nodded.

"*Too* much?"

I shrugged. "It was the Passover, wasn't it? The last plague; the death of the firstborn."

He nodded. "Not exactly how it's taught at Sunday school."

"Miss Robinson never mentioned constructs or vampires."

"I remember her. She had a terrible lisp. Always prattled on about *Jeeffuff* and *Mowffeff*."

I chuckled. "Peter Jones always tried to get her onto Zechariah."

"Yeah. That was a hoot. You just didn't want to stand in front of her when she did, though."

I kicked at a random stone. "How long have you been inside me?"

"Most of your life."

"Yet, you've only started talking to me in the last few months. Why?"

"People see supernatural beings as all-powerful — perpetual motion machines on legs. It's not like that. Not by a long shot. Just like mundane things, supernatural tasks require energy. The greater the event or action, the greater the energy required. We, just like that chap on the cart there or his ox, cannot create energy that we don't already possess. For him to get up and do his daily grind, he needs food and sustenance. Likewise the ox. I, and my kind, are no different."

"Conservation of energy," I said.

Lucifer smiled. "I guess you did listen from time to time at school. Doing what I did, leaving Heaven and inserting myself into you, took a hell of a lot of energy — just about all I had. It took years to regain my strength. I was sat there, powerless, watching you go about your day-today."

"Creepy much."

"But essential. Think of it as having a long-term angel baby," he winked. "You were eating for two." The seraph paused. "What is it?"

"You say that the basic laws of physics apply to everyone?"

He nodded.

"So... what about God?"

My companion shot me a sidelong glance and grinned. "Well, aren't we the quick one? Absolutely! The same rules apply. After God created the Heavenly Realm, He waited for aeons before bringing the basis for all," he gestured around us, "this into existence."

"Okay. I guess."

"But still something's bugging you..."

"I don't know. It feels like it doesn't balance out. Think about it, if a kid draws a picture using a crayon. That crayon becomes the picture, doesn't it? In essence, the crayon is destroyed to make something new. Conservation of energy again. There's only so much to go around."

"Your point?"

"What did God destroy to create the Heavenly Realm?"

Lucifer just shrugged. "I guess you had to be there to see what He dropped into His divine pestle before grinding it up with His all-powerful mortar."

The image of the six-winged figure slicing through reality with the sword flashed into my head and I shuddered. I changed the subject. "It must have been hell. Being inside of me, nearly powerless, that is."

Lucifer seemed to consider this, peering out along the valley below the city walls. "I think I've been through worse and probably will do again." He twisted his lips in a grimace. "You saw Abaddon. In Egypt."

I nodded.

We walked for a while in relative silence. The only noise was the squeaking of the cartwheels in front of us and the grunting of the ox.

"He's my father."

"Is he now?" The three words felt like ice.

"Eloise was pregnant with my sister and me. I could feel his DNA combining with hers."

We walked a little further, Lucifer's hands clenching and unclenching, flames dancing across his knuckles.

"So, how do we explain what we saw in the vision the Abyss showed us of the Indus Valley? *You* were my father there. I've no doubt of that."

"How can you be so sure?"

I reached out with my powers and pushed gently against the whirling torrents of his mind. The vast majority of his thoughts were a hubbub of tempestuous crisscrosses — flashing images passing so quickly that it was impossible to grasp hold of them and apply any kind of interpretation. Between these snatches of speeding recollections were swathes of blackness covered over in what looked like the deepest fog that I had ever encountered. A dark, damp mist hung impenetrably in front of me. It was no wonder that he couldn't make any sense of his memories and the blanks within them. There was, however, one underlying emotion that was unmistakable in the subconscious jumble of his mind. His utter devotion to me. Even if he was not fully aware of its existence, it was there and was what had drawn him to me in the first place.

"I just know," I smiled. "I can feel it."

Lucifer harrumphed. "You're talking like a hormonal

teenager. This isn't some cheap cable soap opera."

"You can feel it too."

The seraph's fiery pupils regarded me over the top of his dark glasses. He nodded in agreement.

"She's playing us."

"The Abyss?"

He nodded again. "She dropped us there so you could see Eloise and Abaddon. She's demonstrating to me that she's the one in control. How could I have been so stupid? There was no way she was going to send us to the Indus and give us all our answers straight away. She wants something."

"What do you think that is?"

The cart in front of us began its final approach to a large gate set in the city wall. Armed soldiers were standing on the entrance road. "I don't know, but right now I think we could do with obscuring."

I nodded, reached out around us and masked our presence as we entered the gates.

"We've moved forward quite a few years."

Lucifer was studying the citizens of the fortified city as we carefully made our way along the bustling streets. All around us, locals went about their day-to-day business, unaware that a boy from the future and an angel from Heaven walked amongst them. Children played games outside their houses. Men chatted over alcoholic beverages. Women performed household chores. A wiry old man dressed in rags was sitting on a street corner, his eyes lightly closed. A pottery cup was positioned on the hard-packed street in front of him. Lucifer flicked his fingers and a coin appeared in his hand. The gold clunked into the pot and the old man raised his hand in what ap-

Child of Light

peared to be a blessing.

It all seemed surreally normal. It may have been numerous centuries before I had been born, but the goings-on was exactly the same as if I had been walking down the street at home.

"How do you know?" I asked with regard to his observation.

We paused in front of what appeared to be a butcher's shop. Some sort of meat hung over a counter and the shop owner was deftly carving a slice off the carcass for a female customer.

"Look at his tools. They're all iron. Where we've just been was definitely Bronze Age. We've jumped forward a few hundred years."

"But, where to?"

"Why don't you find out for us?"

I stared blankly at my companion.

Lucifer pointed to the butcher's head. "Have a peek in here. He'll know where we are."

I nodded and focussed on the ruddy-faced man. Images tumbled over one another as I began to wander around his mind. I ignored the ones of the female customer. It was quite apparent that he had more on his mind than making a profit from the meat he was selling. I saw flashes of twisting streets, of a huge stone building standing tall and proud, rising up from a latticework of scaffolding. Its stonework was second to none, large blocks perfectly set against each other. The man felt incredible pride towards the grand structure and, as his mind radiated warmth at the edifice, I snatched a familiar word out of his otherwise unintelligible language.

"Jerusalem," I said. "We're in Jerusalem. They're just constructing some sort of large building project. A palace? A temple? I'm not sure which."

Lucifer nodded and was about to speak when our attention was drawn to a disturbance up the street. A finely decorated litter, supported by eight burly men and covered in all manner of rich, gaudy-coloured materials, was being paraded along the main thoroughfare. Anxious locals darted off the road, desperate to get out of its way. It drew to a halt next to a certain individual whose eyes bulged wide as he dropped to his knees in the dirt, his hands clasped in a pleading motion before the hidden occupant of the carriage. He spoke rapidly and was quite obviously terrified. As he pleaded before the curtains, his voice climbed up an octave.

Then, without warning, a bolt of lightning shot from the depths of the litter, striking the man square in the chest. He flew across the street and collided with a market stall, shattering earthenware pots and sending the trader's goods scattering across the street. He lay slumped across the bowed table, his mouth gaping open in a deathly rictus.

The next thing I knew, Lucifer was striding toward the litter, flames forming around his fists. My safety bubble must have dropped as the servants screamed when they saw him bearing down upon them. They looked at each other, unsure as to what they should do. They did not want to remain in the path of this frightening creature, but likewise, they did not want to incur the wrath of their master. Lucifer opened his mouth and shouted something at them that sounded like their own language before throwing a number of fireballs at their feet. That sealed the deal and they fled, leaving the opulent form of transport discarded on the stone floor.

A shout arose from within the litter and the curtains

Child of Light

were pulled back as a man emerged, his face at first screwed up in a rage, but then transforming into a mask of terror upon catching sight of Lucifer. He actually took a step back and bumped into the wooden poles that supported the litter.

I gasped, recognising his face as being that of the being whose statues I had seen in Egypt: Asmodeus, the brother of my dark captor.

"You!" he cried out in the same angelic language his brother had used in Egypt and the other angels had spoken in heaven. "How?"

Lucifer cast a slow eye over the litter. The edge of his lips curled in a knowing smile. "Still not mastered riding a horse, I see," he replied in the strange melodious language.

The other man seemed to recover himself slightly, probably from realising that he wasn't being burned to a crisp. "Why should I ride a beast from Cilicia when I can have mortals carry me around? It's far more befitting of my status."

My companion shook his head. "You haven't changed a bit, have you? Right then, Asmodeus, what are you actually up to here?"

As we followed Asmodeus through the twisting streets of Jerusalem, not once did he draw breath from bragging about his various achievements in the city. At first, I was intrigued. Eventually, I was bored. As he prattled on about a certain type of wood that he had procured for a specific item of ornamentation in the Temple, I turned to Lucifer and asked, "You know him, then?"

"He's an angel, like me. Well, not quite. He's an Angeloi, the lowest type."

"He doesn't seem to share that view about his apparent status," I whispered as the low-ranking angel spun a long, convoluted tale about how he had been brought in to replace a Phoenician architect who had been sent by King Hiram, oblivious to the fact that we were ignoring him and talking amongst ourselves. "I saw statues of him in Egypt. They were being torn down and desecrated."

"He'll have done there what he's trying to do here," Lucifer shrugged. "Ingratiate himself to the local nobility, worm his way in like a brain parasite, then slowly turn the state mad. It'll all end in tears, just as it did in Heaven."

"Back before, you had me find out where we were when it's quite obvious you know how to speak the local language. Why?"

"What's the point of having powers if you don't know how to use them?" the seraph smiled before drawing to a sudden halt and staring up at the magnificent edifice in front of us that rose up from the buildings around it. A complex pattern of scaffolding stretched off to the rear of the construction with piles of stone lying in wait to be lifted up into place, but even so, the half-finished structure was far more impressive than any other building I had ever seen. Sharply fashioned stone butted perfectly together, creating a near-seamless smooth white surface that soared into the sky above us. Robed priests smelling of incense and luxurious perfumes climbed the steep steps to a highly decorated portico, offering us polite nods as they entered the building. It appeared that, even though it was not yet fully complete, it was already in use.

"Beautiful, isn't it?" Asmodeus purred as he noted his superior's reaction. The Angeloi paraded through the wide portico into a vast square courtyard. We followed along behind him. "Sol is delighted with my work."

Child of Light

Lucifer raised an eyebrow. "Sol?"

"King Solomon. I told you about him earlier. Do keep up. As I said, he only lets his dearest friends and confidants call him Sol."

I was sure I could hear the seraph mutter, "Good grief," under his breath as he cast his dark glasses around the insides of the structure. I had to admit that, for all Asmodeus' preening and self-congratulatory manner, the Temple really was a sublime work of art. Highly polished wood panelling was surmounted with gold leaf glinting in the sun that shone through the open roof of the courtyard. The delicate aroma of incense seemed to be everywhere. There was no mistaking that this was indeed a very holy place.

I frowned whilst the two angels continued to talk. As Lucifer asked if *she* was here, I was sure that I heard the sound of small footsteps running behind me. I spun around and saw only the priests going about their priestly business: swinging incense burners, staring off piously into the middle distance, guiding an oblivious lamb through a small door to somewhere where there was definitely no nice green grass. The sound came again and I turned once more. I caught a glimpse of white disappearing around the entrance to the courtyard. With a quick glance over my shoulder at the two angels starting to argue, I made after whatever it was that I had seen. As I exited the Temple, I spotted the flash of white again, darting through the crowds and across the road towards a large building opposite. This time, I was also aware of voices, the sound of children laughing, although it seemed to come from within my head rather than from the crowd around me.

I hurried down the steps from the Temple and wove

my way through the crowd. I caught sight of the white again. It was slipping in through the main gate of the large building. I put on some speed and followed it. All the time, the sound of childlike laughter grew in volume in my head. When I entered the room within, I drew to an immediate halt. It was filled with tall pillars of wood that stretched from the floor to the ceiling. The effect was like being in a grove of trees.

"The king calls it his Forest of Lebanon," came a small voice.

I watched as a small girl appeared from behind one of the columns. Had she been human, I would have said that she was about eight years old.

But there was no way that she was even vaguely of this planet. Her long hair was green and her eyes shone like emeralds, olivine mist seeming to drift up from her pupils.

"We like to play in here," she said, smiling.

"We?"

"My sister and I," came another identical voice from another identical girl that stepped out from behind another column. "We play hide and seek around the trees." She frowned, shared a quick look with her sister then asked, "Will you play with us?"

I swallowed. "That depends on the game."

"Oh, we have *lots* of games," said the first of the girls.

"I bet you do." Then something struck me. "Wait a minute. You're talking in English. How's that possible?"

They both shrugged. "It's what you talk," said the second one as she walked towards me, her bare feet padding across the stone floor. "So that's what we talk to you." She cocked her head to one side.

Child of Light

"You've met our mummy," the other one observed. "She finds you…"

"…interesting," finished the second sister. "Are you sure you don't want to play with us?"

I was seriously starting to reconsider my having followed the two creepy little girls when I heard a footstep behind me. "Well, what have we here?" came a familiar voice.

"The Light!" the two squealed in unison. "The Light!" As one, they ran over to Lucifer and began to circle around him, peering up at him, pulling at his clothes and firing questions at him.

"How long are you here?"

"Where were you before here?"

"Have you been *there* yet?"

"Have you met *him* yet?"

"Did you see our mummy?"

"Do you have any sweeties?" At this last question, the two girls stopped their continual walking around the angel and stood together in front of him, regarding him with a certain air of expectancy.

Lucifer smiled and bent down onto one knee so as to be at their face height. "So many questions, little ones. I'm not sure how to answer them all. All except the last one, that is. He flourished his hands in a pair of extravagant circular motions and there in his grip were two purple lollipops. The small girls squeaked in glee and made to grab the sweets, but Lucifer snatched them back. "Now, now, girls. Manners."

"Please may we have the sweeties?" the girls chanted off.

Lucifer grinned. "Utterly adorable aren't they?" Then, to the girls, "You may, as long as you answer a few questions that *I* have. Deal?"

The two looked at each other, nodded, then turned back to face the seraph.

"First, who are you?"

"We are the Potency," one sister replied.

"Asmodeus formed us in Heaven," explained the other. "He drew us from the side of our mummy and fashioned us into a beautiful green stone. Sometimes he wears us as a pretty necklace; other times he lets us run around and play."

My memory flashed back to the statues of the fallen angel in Egypt that had been adorned with the image of a green stone. Lucifer, however, had picked up on something else that they had just mentioned.

"And who would your mummy be?"

"Someone who knows you very well."

"She swims around the three Realms, her song echoing throughout time."

Lucifer raised an eyebrow from behind his sunglasses. "The Abyss?"

The two girls clapped their hands together. "Can we have our sweeties now?"

Lucifer handed the lollipops over and the two sisters took a great delight in sucking on them. "Thank you!" they chimed together around the sweets.

"Not a problem," Lucifer grinned. "Just one more question, though. What is it that you're doing here with Asmodeus?"

The small creatures seemed fit to burst as they bounced maniacally from foot to foot. "Oh, we're having so much fun," one said around her sweet.

"Why don't we show you?" suggested the other.

The girls held out their free hands, which Lucifer

took in his and they led us out of the palace, across the street and up behind the Temple. As I followed behind I couldn't help but smile as the two weird creatures wittered on with boundless enthusiasm about how they were having such fun playing with their toys and how this was much better than being with the big doggies. They hoped that the nice lady would be here soon. They knew she was on her way. She had shown them how to make their toys many years ago and they hoped she would make more with them again. It had been so funny when she had used their toys on the big doggies. It made them laugh and laugh and laugh. Asmodeus liked using their toys, but he was having them do things that were a bit boring, really. They were just moving all the bricks around, building the Temple. They wanted to have more *fun* with their toys. Like they had done in Egypt.

As they said this, something felt rather unsettled in my stomach. I reached for a psychic bottle of ginger cordial.

The unsettled feeling was compounded a hundredfold when we reached the rear of the Temple and there, silently inserting block after block of stone into the growing wall, was a vast army of constructs.

In my head, I watched myself down the whole bottle.

There is something terrifyingly surreal in watching a pair of small girls interacting with and chatting enthusiastically about mindless killing machines as if they are the latest, greatest Barbie dolls. The two little entities bounced around the legs of the constructs as the soulless golems methodically undertook their allotted tasks. The clay creatures hewed gargantuan pieces of stone into necessary sizes, inserted them precisely into exact holes and polished them so that they gleamed iridescently in the Middle Eastern sunshine.

They were unstoppable, unflappable, relentless.

I shuddered at the thought of them being used as an army of foot soldiers.

Apparently, I was not the only one who found their presence somewhat disconcerting.

"You made these?" Lucifer asked the two girls. "How?"

"We drew them up from the ground," one smiled around her purple lollipop.

"It's very easy," said the second.

"We can show you."

Without any further prompting, the two girls turned about-face and held their hands out to a bare patch of ground behind where the clay labourers were working. The air took on an electric feel and their hair started to flow out behind them. Their green eyes flashed brightly and the soil began to move, to undulate. At first, it was a trickle of particles that started to draw together, forming a small blob of earth, but then it erupted up like a tree trunk, bursting fully formed from the ground beneath. There was a wet noise as arms stretched out from the broad clay pole and a wide mouth broke the smooth consistency of its surface. Its base split as it took an unsteady step forward before stamping down hard on the ground and standing to attention in front of us, a complete construct.

Lucifer let a low whistle escape his lips. He approached the golem and peered at it over the top of his glasses with an inquisitive intensity. "Fascinating," he whispered. "Truly fascinating." He reached out a finger and touched the creature's *skin*. He smiled as he pulled

Child of Light

the digit back and saw an imprint of his fingertip remaining in the damp clay. "Does it tire you out making these?"

"Not at all," replied one of the girls.

"We can make as many as you want," said the other.

Lucifer looked across at them, his head cocked slightly to one side.

"And you'll want a lot…" said the first.

The seraph crossed his denim-clad arms across his chest. "Will I now? What makes you say that?"

"One day, in the future…" The little girl paused and frowned. "*Your* future… You'll want a whole army of these."

"Will I indeed…?" The seraph turned his attention back to the newly formed construct, then to the army of workers, before settling once more on the new creation, his fiery eyes peering up at its blank, eyeless face. "I have to say, they look somewhat *basic*. Can they be modified?"

The girls nodded in unison. "We created this one for you."

"All you have to do is touch it and it will change into what you want."

The edge of Lucifer's mouth curled up just a touch. "Well, I'm not sure Asmodeus would like me to do that. Not one little bit." He reached out and slapped his hand firmly on the construct. The creature's surface began to ripple and stretch as an idea of shape began to take form. Patterns eddied and rolled as if their designer was running through numerous variations, trying them out for size. Eventually, the surface began to solidify into something quite different to how it had started out. It was still the same rough size and build, but rather than possessing the identical domed, neckless top as was shared by its kin, it rolled a large head around on its new shoulders. Two slits popped open on its face through which black eyeballs peered and a pair of nostrils opened up on a squashed, snout-like nose. Its mouth shrunk in size and snaggle teeth slid into view along its thick lips. Its broad arms took on a humanoid musculature, as did its torso and its legs. Clothing similar to the armour we had seen worn by the guards at the main gate to the city formed across its naked body. The being stretched its arms up above its large head, cracked its joints and ran its fingers down what appeared to be a simulacrum of a burnished metal helmet.

It turned its head to Lucifer, opened its mouth and a booming voice enquired, "Who am I?"

"You know what, my friend," Lucifer replied, "that's a question I've been asking myself quite a bit lately as well." He crossed his arms and tapped an index finger against his lips. "Tell you what. I think you look like a Gog. How about that? You like the name *Gog*?"

The construct's thick brow knitted in thought before it slowly nodded.

Lucifer clapped his hands together. "Excellent! Oh, in that case…" He took a few steps backwards before holding out his right hand. A small flame began to dance in the upturned palm. It bounced and flickered over the seraph's skin until forming into a small pink cube that appeared to be dusted with fine sugar. "Well, Gog, as it's technically your birthday, here's a little present for you. It's a small piece of Turkish delight. I hope you have a sweet tooth."

The newly-born construct peered over at the sweet in the seraph's hand.

"Go on," Lucifer urged. "Take it. Show me what you

Child of Light

can do."

Gog looked down at his own immense hand before lifting his arm to shoulder height and reaching out for the sweet. The muscular limb stretched to twice the length of an average-sized human before his fingers wrapped around the delicacy and his muscles snapped back to their original form. Lucifer chuckled to himself as he observed the elastic transformation of the construct's arm.

With his arm back to its original length, Gog gave the Turkish delight a cautious sniff before popping the candy in his mouth. As he chewed, his eyes lit up with glee. "I like. You have more?"

"Sorry, friend," Lucifer shook his head. "It's the wrong place, wrong time. That," he smiled as he wiped the remains of the sugar from his hand, "was just an illusion. A very clever one I might add." The fire in his pupils flared briefly. "Tell you what, one day, in the future, I'll bring you some of the real stuff, when it's actually being made. You'd like that?"

Gog nodded with enthusiasm and Lucifer smiled. My companion's eyes wandered back over to the silent army of clay builders. "One more question," he asked the two girls, "how long has all this taken so far?"

"Not long," one replied.

"Exactly?"

"Four days," replied the other. "They're just working on the back of it now. Then they'll be finished."

Lucifer crossed his arms and tapped his chin with his index finger. "When it's finished, what's going to happen to the *workforce*?"

The two girls shared a surreptitious glance and then beamed as they said, "Asmodeus said that we'd be able to play with them. He promised."

The seraph pursed his lips. "Of course he did," he muttered under his breath. "Well, tell you what," he smiled at the girls as he patted Gog on one of his immense shoulders, "for now, why don't you two go and play with our new friend here?"

The twins bounced up and down with glee before slipping their hands into those of the newborn construct, chattering away about all the fun things that wanted to do. Unfortunately (or, perhaps, fortunately) I didn't hear what they had in mind for their new plaything as a shout of rage obscured their voices.

"What have you done!" Asmodeus stormed into the building site, uncontrolled electricity sparking from his hands. "What is *that*?"

"Not sure yet," Lucifer grinned. "He's on a voyage of self-discovery. Something that will be far more frequent in a few thousand years but normally accompanied by mellowing narcotics."

"No! Destroy it! Get rid of it!" the Angeloi ranted. "You can't do that!"

I gasped as he was lifted off his feet by unseen hands and thrown against the wall of the Temple. His eyes widened in fear as Lucifer turned on him. "No one tells me what I can or can't do," the seraph growled. "Certainly, not you." He raised a fist and it erupted into flame.

Asmodeus frantically shook his head from side to side. "Please. Please, no. Please. Not that. You know what it'll do to me. It'll send me *there*."

Lucifer drew his fist back in order to hurl a destructive fireball at the wretch but halted his action as trumpets began to sound from around the other side of the building. He frowned, seemed to focus on something that I could not perceive, then groaned, "You've got to be kidding me…"

I almost had to run to keep pace with the two angelic beings as they hurried around to the front of the temple. Lucifer had given no explanation for his comment and had set straight off without a word; Asmodeus had scurried along behind him, his gaudily coloured robes trailing in the dirt of the construction site. Behind me, the newly-birthed construct ambled happily along, a small, green-haired girl attached to each hand.

The sight that met my eyes as I rounded the building reminded me of a film I had watched at a friend's house one Easter holiday when I was still in primary school. I can't remember the title, but it was a very grand affair from the 1950s, I think. Richard Burton was in it (my friend's mum was seriously into him) and it was set in Rome with lavish sets and hundreds of extras all decked out in togas and the like. Atop the grand steps to the front of the Temple (the one in front of me, not the one in front of my mate's mum's screen idol) stood a grand entourage of individuals. There were armour-clad soldiers, aristocrats wearing expensive robes, bare-chested slaves and, in the middle of all of these, upon a grand chair underneath a pure white canopy, was seated a middle-aged man wearing so much jewellery that I thought it would be impossible for him to move under the weight of the raiment.

Asmodeus strode right up to the man and started to talk to him in the human's own language. Amongst the babble of words, I just about managed to catch the name Sol a few times. I leaned across to Lucifer: "The king himself, then?"

The seraph nodded slowly as he listened to the

conversation. "Old Sparky is asking Solomon what the commotion is. It would appear that the king has received word that a special guest has just arrived on the outskirts of the city."

I studied the face of my companion. I noted the way the seraph's lips twisted together. "You know who it is?"

Lucifer nodded an affirmation and turned to face a rising commotion as, along the main thoroughfare to the Temple, the most amazing procession came into view. There were soldiers on horses, riding in accompaniment to a troop of five or six elephants that were all laden down with what appeared to be a plethora of goods and wares. Eight camels followed, similarly decked out. There was even a giraffe with multicoloured ribbons entwined around its graceful neck. The whole city was an uproar of music and fanfare as drummers preceded the entourage, pounding out a regular beat in time to the steady footfalls of the elephants whilst trumpeters blew with all their might to announce the arrival of someone of the greatest of importance.

This someone followed up the rear of the cavalcade, atop a pure white elephant, the skin of which had been elegantly painted with all manner of glyphs and symbols. The person of the utmost wealth and nobility was being carried in a curtained compartment, its blue fabrics drifting lazily in the breeze.

"Always a showoff," Lucifer sighed and explained: "The colour blue was incredibly hard to manufacture in this period. To have so much fabric in that particular hue is an overwhelming statement of wealth and importance." He shook his head. "But then, I would expect nothing else from *her*."

I was about to ask who *she* was, but my question

Child of Light

was obliterated by the sound of ceremonial trumpets blaring out once more from the convoy. I winced as twenty tall, vertical golden horns with serpentine mouths filled the surrounding area with a cacophony of noise. The white elephant drew level with the entrance to the temple and an official dismounted from a horse that he rode next to the pachyderm. He approached the foot of the steps and knelt in respect before the king. Solomon nodded his head and waved for the man to rise. The man spoke loud and clear, announcing his Mistress.

"For many miles, across treacherous land and wilderness," Lucifer translated, "my mistress has travelled in search of the famed wisdom of the King of Israel. She humbly begs an audience with your greatness and has brought a multitude of lavish gifts as a sign of her respect for your majesty."

Solomon asked something in return. "He's asking who this mysterious woman is," Lucifer whispered, then continued as the servant of the still-concealed guest replied, "She is a ruler in her own right, in her beautiful land far, far away. A land overflowing with riches that she wishes to share with you and your kingdom. She is… *good grief…* a beauty the like of which this world has never known. Shrewd in politics and," Lucifer stifled a laugh, "always accepting of new cultures. I give you… the Queen of Sheba."

Upon the announcement of the mysterious woman's title, the blue curtains on the carriage parted, seemingly by themselves, and revealed a majestic woman standing, looking down at the congregated nobility and royalty before her. Her hair was long and dark, flowing over a diaphanous dress that left just enough to the imagination to be vaguely decent. Her tanned skin was immaculate, without blemish, and her lips were painted a bright red, matching the vibrant colour of the nails on her hands, which she held out in front of her. Slowly, she rotated her slender wrists and water miraculously began to flow from her hands, streaming down to the steps below. The liquid eddied and swirled before coalescing into a flight of stairs down which the Queen of Sheba gracefully stepped, her dress spreading out behind her, allowing each step to reveal her shapely legs. When she reached the Temple steps, she clicked her fingers and the watery staircase evaporated into steam.

A cruel smile spread across her face as the whole courtyard stood or sat in stunned silence. All, that was except for Lucifer. "Never changes. It's always me, me, me; look at me."

"Who is she?" I asked.

"That," replied the seraph, "is the fallen angel Asherah." He sighed. "Which means trouble."

The supposed queen had just placed one foot on the stairs to the Temple when there was an outcry from the midst of the surrounding populace of Jerusalem. The crowds were pushed aside and a roughly dressed man barged his way forwards. I recognised him as the beggar to whom Lucifer had tossed the gold coin when we had entered the city. He was the polar opposite of the priests and nobles that stood with Solomon at the pinnacle of the staircase. Whereas they were groomed, washed and sported neatly styled hair, he was bedraggled and dressed in rags. His untamed hair contained strands of straw and, as he drew closer, I was sure there was the occasional living insect amongst his wild curls.

He was clearly not pleased with the new arrival in town. Marching over to the foot of the steps, he cried out in his native tongue as he waved his staff fashioned from a rough branch in front of him. He pointed and shouted at Asherah, then turned to the royal retinue and asked something of Solomon.

"What's going on?" I asked Lucifer.

"It appears that this is some sort of local holy man, a devotee of Yahweh," my companion explained. "He's claiming that the Queen of Sheba is here to pollute the new temple with her pagan ways. He's demanding that Solomon refuse her shiny trinkets and sends her packing.

"Not really a good idea."

"Why? You think the king will be cross with him?"

Lucifer shook his head. "Not the king."

And then I heard it, a soft tune drifting across the concourse. The subtle melody slipped its way over the square, weaving a path through all who stood there. Every person it passed shifted awkwardly, uncomfortably, as if someone had just peered into their deepest, darkest fantasy. The song slithered over the pristine stone paving, increasing in volume as it homed in on its target. It shot forward, seeking out the harsh complaints of the hermit. The elderly man seemed to twitch and slap at his arms and his chest as the ever-complex harmony snaked around him, wrapping his angry protests in strong coils until his words stuttered to a bemused halt. He lifted his face to the beautiful woman who stood before him, her red, beguiling lips moving in time to the insidious tune. She raised a hand and with a long, slender finger beckoned him to come to her. The hermit grimaced and, as his left foot jerked an involuntary step forward, he cried out in surprise. His brow creased as he fought the fallen angel's command, but her will was absolute, unable to be defied. His treacherous legs carried him to her presence.

No one said a word as the volume and intensity of the song increased tenfold. Its melody echoed around the square in front of the Temple, its notes reverberating off the stone walls. Standing where I was, at the back of the crowd, even I was affected by her hypnotic tune. In my head, I saw visions of opulent palaces and grand temples, wooden poles decorated with colourful ribbons, as beads of sweat pearled on my skin. The hermit, in the very epicentre of her melodic tempest, did not stand a chance.

His knees buckled and, with a loud groan, he slumped onto the floor before the supposed queen. I waited and expected her to give the command for him to kiss her feet, to show his devotion to her.

What she actually asked for was far more brutal.

The angel muttered something in the holy man's tongue and her finger pointed to a crude knife that was tucked in his belt. The old man grimaced as his hand snapped to the hilt of the weapon. His lips pulled back and his teeth were clenched together as he drew the knife and did the unthinkable. He drove it into his own chest.

But the torture did not stop there.

As he screamed in agony, he drew the blade upwards and sliced a wide gash in his torso. Then, as blood flowed down his grubby sackcloth, he reached into his chest and ripped out his heart, holding it up to the cruel beauty in front of him before collapsing dead at her feet. His still-beating organ slipped out of his slack hand and rolled in front of her sandalled foot. Asherah looked down at the bloody mess with disgust, raised her foot and ground the heart into the dirt with her heel. Then, fixing a smile on her face, she proceeded up the stairs to Solomon leaving the body of the hermit where it lay, forgotten, no longer important.

Child of Light

There was a feast — a rather opulent one indeed. Apart from the overflowing dishes of olives, most of the food I could not identify, but I believe there was quite a bit of goat and even some veal. Solomon made a big show of Asherah as his guest of honour, much to the annoyance of Asmodeus, who seemed to have seriously had his sycophantic nose put out of joint. He sat a few seats away from the king, glowering into his drink whereas the so-called queen was seated at the monarch's right hand, apparently hanging on the ruler's every word as he regaled her with grand stories of how he had secured his kingdom and had eliminated all the threats to his throne. He boasted that even now he was planning on building the greatest fortification the land had ever seen at Megiddo, to ensure his grip on his father's legacy did not weaken. He had already instructed that the existing settlement there be cleared of its population and, once the Temple was complete, work would begin on the strongest fort that the world had ever known. If Asherah was bored by this bout of regal bragging, it did not show. Not once did she interrupt the monarch. In fact, she would occasionally prompt him to continue, asking him to elaborate on the smallest of details, much to the delight of the King of Israel.

Lucifer and I were seated down at the far end of the banqueting table, fairly much keeping ourselves to ourselves. We had just mingled with the crowd as they had processed over to Solomon's palace and, without much real effort, had managed to secure ourselves places at the banquet.

Asherah kept glancing down at us, or more precisely at Lucifer. Every time she did, there was a distinct worried look in her eye, but this was not noticed by our host who just enjoyed the constant attention of the beautiful woman.

As the feast began to wind down, Lucifer disappeared for a short while before returning and saying that he had secured us some rooms for the night in the palace. I didn't ask how as, quite frankly, I was bushed and in need of sleep. I followed him out of the banqueting hall and, as I did, I got a distinct feeling that I was being watched. I turned and looked down to the head of the table where Solomon was regaling Asherah with some sort of tall tale that was causing him much amusement. The fallen angel's attention, however, was elsewhere. She held a golden goblet to her red lips and, as she slowly sipped the dark wine, her eyes were firmly fixed upon me, small flames dancing intriguingly in her pupils. I could not help but feel like a rabbit confronted by an apex predator.

There was a tug on my elbow. "Come on," Lucifer urged, guiding me out into the corridor. "Trust me, you want to keep as great a distance as possible between you and her."

I let out a sharp breath and fell in pace next to the seraph. "I have to say, I wholeheartedly agree. She is…" I shrugged, lost for words.

"There are many adjectives one could use to describe the Lady of the Sea. Not one of them is polite." After saying this, Lucifer appeared to fall into a contemplative silence, his hands thrust into the pockets of his denim jacket.

"What is it?"

"Hmmm?"

"You seem distracted."

He shook his head as we climbed some stairs to

the upper level of the palace. At the top of the staircase, we emerged onto a balcony that provided a view of the Temple and the rest of the sprawling city. Down below, lights flickered in the dark as guards patrolled the narrow streets. Beyond the city walls, there was complete and utter blackness."

"It's quite something," I commented.

"Quite the marvel of its time," Lucifer agreed. "And yet, in the age in which you live, none of this will remain."

I frowned. "But Jerusalem still exists and, from what I know, it's even bigger than this."

"True, but it's not *this* Jerusalem." He placed his hands on the stone balcony and leaned out over the city, inhaling the exotic scents of the sleeping conurbation. "The city you see before you in the here and now will have been destroyed numerous times. It will be laid desolate and bare. Foreign powers will assault it and flatten it into the earth. Not even Asmodeus' great wonder will remain. All the stonework will be broken down, recycled and reused. Its treasures will be pillaged, carried off to foreign countries and melted down to become idols of foreign deities.

"And it will all be the fault of Asmodeus and Asherah."

"How come?"

"You've seen how they are, lording it over all and sundry. They waltz in and present themselves as great beings, sometimes even gods, that can lift society out of the dirt." He shook his head. "Even now, in the darkness of the night, workmen are down there erecting *asherim* in her honour. They will be levelling earth in the high places to make her a *bamot*." The seraph grunted in disgust. "Then, when the two of them have had enough, they'll wander off to the next sucker. But their worshippers will continue to think that they will still be around to protect them, to save them from the ravening hordes. As a result, the populace left behind is never fully prepared for when the inevitable assault comes, when the enemy is at the gates or in their midst.

"And this becomes the curse of humanity.

"It is never prepared, never ready. It always thinks that someone else will save it.

"Someone needs to teach it to stand up for itself; to be prepared. It needs to recognise the signs when the enemy approaches and to stand firm and fight for its very survival."

"Could you do that?"

The seraph raised an eyebrow behind his dark glasses. "Me?" he chuckled. "Whoever would listen to the angel that defied God Himself? Even by this period in history, they are starting to demonise concepts such as Death and Destruction." He pointed out over the edge of the city wall. "You see that valley there? It's called Gehinnom. It simply means "Valley of the son of Hinnom". A rather sweet name, you'd think, yet, in just a couple of generations, things will have travelled so far south here that they will be sacrificing children there to a deaf god in a vain attempt to save their city. From that point forward, the valley will be infamous as a place of bloodshed. It will be synonymous with Hell."

"Why… Why doesn't…?" I trailed off as Lucifer faced me.

"Why doesn't God intervene?"

I nodded.

"Why should He?"

"He's a God of love, of compassion. Surely it must

hurt Him to see all this bloodshed?"

"I'm sure it does. But what should He do? Should He smite the evildoers? Should He walk seven leagues to trample upon the heathen? If He did that, then He would be wiping out people who are just as much part of His creation as those He is trying to protect. His ways are more subtle. He speaks to those who will listen and encourages them to teach their kindred about the right path, a path of love and kindness. Then, you know what happens when those good souls try to spread His message? They're stoned, burned, shot and nailed to a cross." He turned away from me and quickly rubbed a finger at the corner of his right eye. "No. Humanity must learn how to fight, but not itself. It has to fight to survive."

We remained in Jerusalem for a week, keeping to the shadows of society, observing the political goings-on from the neutral, objective sidelines. Whereas the people of the city spent the seven days in feasting and jubilation, both at the completion of the Temple and the visitation of the Queen of Sheba, we witnessed changes around the city: some subtle, some not.

I spent a good part of my time listening to the locals speaking and gleaning images from their minds as they did so. This meant that I was able to pick up a basic grasp of their language with an agreeable rapidity. The main topic of conversation was the mysterious regal visitor who now seemed to have their king in her thrall. Opinions on the queen were definitely mixed. Some welcomed her as a breath of fresh air, most suited to the new regime and a time of peace and prosperity. They saw her as heralding a new age of wealth and luxury that would trickle down to the lower reaches of the population. It was noticeable that the wealthier women in the city started to model their fashion sense on hers, wearing far more revealing outfits than when we had first arrived. Also, there seemed to be a sudden abundance of exotic foods available from the street vendors, all attached to exotic price tags to match.

Not all opinions on the flamboyant monarch were positive. There were grumblings about the not-so-subtle changes that she had brought about. As Lucifer had predicted, a number of *bamot* had been constructed around the city — high place groves full of *asherim*, wooden poles that paid homage to the pagan goddess of the Canaanites. The more conservative members of the populace decried these rapid construction projects and resolutely stated that Yahweh would not stand for such idolatrousness and would pour down his wrath upon the city. To me though, they were reminiscent of Solomon's Forest of Lebanon. The elegant poles were surely not too dissimilar to the grand barren trees that he had standing sentinel in his own palace? Perhaps the Canaanite practices and beliefs were already seeded in the Israelite culture? All they needed were just a fresh watering in order to encourage them to grow and blossom.

One thing that definitely upset the crowd was Asmodeus' knee-jerk reaction to the love of all things Asherah. Three days into our stay, in fact, the day that the Temple was due to be completed, Solomon's high priest stormed up to the fallen angel in the middle of the street and berated him for the sudden appearance of the *pagan sites* that had sprung up around town more or less overnight. His face practically turned purple as he violently jabbed the architect of the Temple in the chest, stating that the building had become a laughing stock and that the king should have stuck with the original Phoenician designs rather than bringing in someone whom no one had ever heard of. "If it had been built properly, by human hands," the priest declared, "then the locals would have more respect for it, rather than deserting the true God for some pagan poles."

Asmodeus did not take the criticism well.

That afternoon, after the charred remains of the angry priest were scraped up off the stone floor, a great ceremony of pomp and majesty was held as the final stone was set in place in the towering place of worship. The new high priest led his decidedly anxious brethren in a ceremony of dedication as Asmodeus had his constructs install in the Temple's open courtyard two gigantic stone pillars. Atop each was a massive bronze brazier which, upon completion, burned with sweet-smelling incense. The angelic architect made a great show of their first use and proclaimed, much to the bemusement of the surrounding priests, that they were named *Jachin* and *Boaz*. As the attendant dignitaries and royal hangers-on clapped and applauded their sycophantic (and let's face it, decidedly worried and probably terrified) praise, Asherah just glowered in anger, Lucifer groaned and rolled his eyes.

"What is it?"

"Trouble," he growled. "Little Sparky is trying to wrench favour back from the hands of his partner in crime. These," he nodded to the two towering incense burners, "can be found throughout Egypt and Canaan. He told *Sol*," it was impossible to miss the derision in his voice, "that they're representations of the pillars of fire and cloud that guided the Children of the Hebrews out of Egypt. They're actually dedications to the gods Osiris and Ba'al, both of whom are personifications of Asmodeus.

He's definitely done a one-up on Asherah's handiwork. She may dominate the surrounding city with her *asherim,* but this is a statement, loud and proud, that the Temple and the authority of Solomon belong to Asmodeus.

"She won't take that well. When the bubbles of large egos are burst, they make a hell of a noise."

It didn't take long for the Angeloi to prove the seraph right. As the crowd dispersed and the priests properly settled into their new base of operations, whilst keeping a discreet distance from its mercurial builder, Asherah stormed up to Asmodeus and began to harangue her fellow angel in their native tongue.

Lucifer shook his head and headed over to the squabbling couple. "Look at the pair of you," he said, "bickering like a pair of infants over which one pissed in the sand pit. I mean, really, I just don't get it. A whole planet and you have to follow each other around causing chaos wherever you set foot." They both opened their mouths to protest, but the seraph's raised hand silenced them. "You're quite obviously miserable. Anyone with half a brain can see that. You lived in paradise, for crying out loud! Yet you threw it all away." He shook his head. "Do you even remember what it was like there? The peace? The tranquillity? I bet you don't. You'll have reshaped your memories to your own liking. You'll have set yourselves as poor dramatic heroes who were downtrodden and enslaved to some higher being. You'll see your act of running away as a blessed escape." He snorted in contempt. "What's the betting that in a few thousand years you'll do the same to this little escapade? Rather than recalling the arguing and backbiting, you'll look back on this moment and see yourselves as being adored by the masses and feeling content with all you've accomplished.

Child of Light

"You never realised just how good you had it, did you?" And, with a deep sigh, the seraph turned and walked off into the city. I turned and followed him, but not before I saw the looks on the faces of the sulking angels.

One thing was for sure; this wasn't over.

One thing we did *not* witness during our stay was any evidence of our mode of temporal transport. By our sixth day in Jerusalem, it was quite obvious that Lucifer was becoming concerned. He was far snappier than normal. His usual dry wit and normal passive observance were becoming increasingly replaced with a sharp tongue and a fiery temper as he seemed to constantly pace the streets of the city as if looking for some sort of exit that was hidden from our view. More than once, I overheard him muttering to himself, "Why are we here? What the hell does she want from us?"

I could not mistake the feeling of the seraph that the Abyss was manipulating us just as much as Asherah and Asmodeus were manipulating the King of Israel.

The bizarrely human manifestation of the living waters that constantly snaked their way around the universe finally made an appearance on our seventh night in Jerusalem.

I had been struggling to get to sleep. The rooms that Lucifer had acquired for us were incredibly luxurious (it was a royal palace, after all) and my bed was large enough to sleep an army, but the heat of that final night we were there was stifling. Every time I felt my eyes drift shut with fatigue, a hot flush would cause me to groan, turn over and kick more of the fine cotton bedding off my sweat-sodden body. This happened six times without incident. Each time I would grunt in frustration, thump my pillows and repeat the ritual of one more accustomed to sleeping in cooler climes.

It was on the seventh attempt at sleep that she appeared.

"You are restless," came the voice of the teenage girl.

"Your destiny weighs heavy on your mind," stated the middle-aged woman.

"You do not understand who you are," explained the old hag.

My eyes snapped open and I saw immediately that I was no longer knotted up in discarded sheets. I was lying on cold earth that was dotted with scant patches of brown, withered grass. I leapt to my feet, all weariness dispelled from me by shock and a pounding heart.

I glanced down and ran my hands over my body before breathing a sigh of relief that at least I appeared to be clothed.

The teenage girl stood staring at me, her watery clothes undulating and sparking with small fires in their ripples.

"Where am I?"

"Where I wish you to be."

My eyes scanned my surroundings. I was definitely no longer in Israel. There were hills in the distance; rolling ones covered in the same patchy grass that lay round about me. Dying trees hung desolately at the side of a rutted track that led off seemingly for miles. The middle-aged woman turned and began to walk along the path. I shook my head and followed.

"But where exactly would that be? Where's Lucifer?"

"You are so young," the cracked voice of the old

Child of Light

woman said, "yet carry so much weight."

"There are things you should see," the girl continued.

"Things of which you should be aware," completed the middle-aged woman.

"What I'm aware of," I snapped, "is that you seem to be just using us as playthings."

"You think this is a game?" asked the crone.

"What else could it be for you? You know everything! What sort of existence could that be? Where is the real... *living*?" I huffed in exasperation. "I know for sure that I wouldn't want it. Every day would be so dull as you'd already know what was going to happen. What's worse, you'd know how it was all going to end."

The girl was silent.

The woman said nothing.

The crone looked away.

I nodded. "And it terrifies you, doesn't it? The simple fact that, with all your omniscience, all your power, at some point you will be swept away. How will it happen? What will be the fate of the mighty Abyss?"

The watery eyes of the girl glared up at me. "You are truly your father's son."

"Yet you possess so much of your mother," finished the woman.

I steadied myself, keeping my anger in check. "And what of my sister? What is *she* like?"

A small smile touched the lips of the crone. "The same, yet different."

I ran my fingers through my bed-head hair. "Look, I know you're doing whatever it is you're doing with all..." I gestured wildly around us at the barren landscape, "*this*, but can you please answer just one question for me?

What's her name?"

The girl's eyes narrowed somewhat. "Amanda. Her name is Amanda."

"And, together, you will achieve great things," whispered the woman. The air in front of me shifted and turned, as if someone was remoulding it. When it settled, I saw a moving image of my sister, but she was older than I had seen before. She looked to be about my age.

She was also apparently furious.

Amanda was storming down a narrow corridor, a dark glower on her face. I couldn't help but notice that the building was erupting in flame behind her. The image widened momentarily and I saw balls of fire surrounding her hands which she dragged along the walls in her wake.

The image twisted again and snapped shut.

I was left with a smile on my face. "It would appear she takes after our father."

"Beware," warned the crone, ignoring my comment and pointing a gnarled finger up into the air, "your paths are perilous and great dangers lie ahead."

The air around me was rent with a deafening noise. I turned to face the sound and watched in stupefaction as two dragons appeared from behind the hills.

One was red with seven heads.

One was obsidian black.

They screamed in high-pitched tones as they clawed and slashed continually at each other. As the red one struck the black, gouts of crimson blood fell to the floor. When the liquid struck the desolate ground, it formed into an army of constructs. As the black struck the red, droplets of fire burst from the scarlet dragon's wounds and seared the ground below, before taking the form of creatures like the vampires I had seen in Egypt.

Child of Light

The opposing armies advanced upon each other and began to fight. It was like no battle I had ever seen on the History Channel. Vampires screamed as constructs impaled them with lances; constructs withered to dust as vampires drained them by using their wickedly sharp fangs. And all the time, above the melee, the two dragons continued to fight, causing more and more pawns to be sent into a fruitless battle.

"What is this?" I managed, forcing down the sickening revulsion in my stomach.

"This is what is," said the girl.

"This is what has always been," said the woman.

"*This*, is what will become," said the crone as she waved her gnarled hand, causing the sight in front of me to change. The hills and the gruesome battle faded, being replaced with the shadowy outline of a church spire.

I frowned as the building took on a more solid shape. It was old, incredibly old. The stone was chipped and worn. The roof seemed to have been smashed at some point by an incredibly strong force. Around the Gothic structure was a wide lake that looked impassable without a boat.

"What is this?" I asked.

"Find your sister," said the girl, ignoring my question.

"You must protect her at all costs," said the woman.

"From her womb will be born the future of humanity and its past," stated the crone.

"This is the place where Kanor dwells," explained the girl.

"You must avoid this place at all costs," said the woman.

"Why?"

The crone's watery eyes held me fast. "It is the place where you will die at the hands of the Black Dragon."

I awoke with a start, my heart thumping in my bare chest.

"My, my," came a curious feminine voice from the darker depths of my room. "Someone was having a dream. Was it a *nice* one?"

My eyes darted around the gloom and finally located a shadow near the door. The shapely silhouette parted company with the wall and Asherah stalked gracefully across to my bed. She wore a long white cotton gown that seemed to accentuate her every curve with each step that she took toward me. I instinctively made to grab my bedding, to cover myself up, but my hands froze as my fingertips touched the rumpled sheets. The fallen angel smiled wickedly as her siren song began to fill the room.

My heart continued to thump against my ribs, but it was no longer a beating of fear. I heard a longing groan escape my mouth.

Asherah grinned as she slid up onto my bed. Her pupils burned bright with fire in the darkness of the room before she slowly closed her eyelids and inhaled deeply. "Mmm… Something smells good!" she moaned. Her eyes snapped open once more. "What are you?" Reaching out, she tracked a finely manicured nail down my cheek and she leaned in, her exotic perfume overwhelming my senses as she placed a soft kiss on my perspiring forehead. "Something about you is so… *powerful*. I need a taste."

Okay, I don't want to say too much here, because, well, it's rather embarrassing, but let's just say that my body reacted the way that many male bodies would in this situation.

Asherah was rather pleased with this autonomic response. She continued to smile as she ran first her smooth fingertips, then her wet lips, over the curve of my shoulder. "You are truly fascinating," she murmured softly between the kisses. "Who are you? Why are you with *him*?" She pulled back, her face directly in front of mine. I was stupefied, unable to speak. All I wanted right then was for her lips to touch mine. "I think," she mused as her hand pressed against my pounding chest, pushing me back onto the bedding, "that you ought to *fill me in...*"

The fallen angel cast away any remnant of bedding and was about to climb on top of me when the room was suddenly lit up with a crackling display of lightning. She screamed in shock and agony as she was catapulted off the bed and onto the floor. Her siren song cut short, I gasped hot air down into my lungs and adrenaline surged through my body, purging my senses of her spell.

Asherah sprung to her feet and turned to face the entrance to my room, balls of water coalescing around her fists. Her long hair snaked wildly around her head. "How dare you!" she screamed at the intruder in the doorway.

I did the only thing that I could at that moment. I drew my protective bubble around myself and hid in embarrassment.

Asmodeus was about to throw a retort back but paused upon apparently witnessing a naked teenage boy vanish into thin air. "Solomon wants to see us," he eventually snapped, electricity still dancing across his knuckles. He glared across the room at the dishevelled bed. "*All* of us..."

I threw my clothes on in what I hoped resembled some sort of presentable order and scurried out of the room behind the two fallen angels. Asherah glided through the passageways with not a single hair out of place or even the slightest look of worry on her beautiful face; Asmodeus looked fit to electrocute anyone who dared get in his way. Fortunately, for the palace staff, our journey to Solomon's throne room was unimpeded and the King of Israel would not be having to replace any barbecued servants.

The first shadow of doubt passed across Asherah's face when we entered the grand room where Solomon was sitting upon an imposing carved throne that was covered completely in gold leaf. It was not the presence of the king that caused her to pause, but the person who was standing behind him.

Lucifer was poised nonchalantly with one hand resting on the back of the king's seat of power. As usual, his eyes were obscured by his dark sunglasses, but the curve of his lips betrayed an amusement that was not shared by the two other angels.

Asherah opened her mouth to speak but the king imperiously raised a silencing hand. "It has come to my attention, that things are not what they seem."

The fallen angels shot each other a sidelong glance. There was no mistaking the threatening menace in the king's voice. I watched as two pairs of hands twitched, one sparking electricity, one twisting water droplets across its knuckles. I swallowed. It was obvious that the two were readying themselves for a showdown.

The hand perched on the back of Solomon's throne erupted into flame. Lucifer didn't move a muscle. He just kept smiling straight ahead as the glow from his fiery digits flickered across the room.

The two fallen angels quickly reined in their own elemental powers.

Lucifer nodded and extinguished his fiery hand.

"I have been informed," continued Solomon as he pointed to the Potency that Asmodeus currently wore on a chain around his neck, "that this stone you possess has the ability to bring about the ruin of not only my kingdom but of all civilisation."

Asmodeus opened his mouth to protest but a slight shake of Lucifer's head silenced any words before they escaped his mouth.

"I also believe that it is a weapon that cannot be destroyed due to its... *unnatural*... properties. However, measures must be undertaken to ensure that it can never be wielded in a destructive fashion. It is to be rent in two and the halves are to be hidden in the farthest reaches of the planet."

This time, no manner of threat from the seraph could prevent Asmodeus from crying out in protest. However, his shout went unheeded as Lucifer held out his free hand and the chain around the Angeloi's neck snapped as the Potency flew across the throne room into the seraph's grasp.

What occurred next happened in a blur.

Asmodeus screamed out in rage and launched himself at Lucifer. Guards stepped forward and blocked his way momentarily. As the Angeloi battered and shocked his way through the soldiers, Lucifer took the Potency in both hands and began to apply pressure to the stone. As he did so, he paused and the fires in his eyes burned with an intensity I had yet to witness. He stared down into the depths of the green stone, which seemed to undulate and pulse in his grip, a green smoke drifting up from its surface. In my head, I heard a three-fold rhythm play over and over as words were repeated, echoing around my skull:

"We are one...
"We are one...
"We are one..."

Asmodeus broke through the guards, after making their corpses dance with innumerate voltage, and lunged at the Potency. Just as he reached out to grab back his prize possession, Lucifer snapped out of his trance and spun his wrists in opposite directions. The stone fractured with a deafening crack and the threefold rhythm in my head was replaced with the screams of a small girl. I was obviously not the only one to hear this as everyone in the room dropped to their knees with their hands over their ears in a vain attempt to block out the cacophony of wailing. Lucifer, as he did so, dropped the two halves of the Potency. Asmodeus forced himself to recover, held out a hand and snatched one half up before disappearing with a loud crack. A second cracking noise followed and I was aware that Asherah had also disappeared.

Lucifer recovered his composure, stepped over to the remaining green hemisphere and scooped it up.

Silence descended upon the throne room.

Silence, that was, apart from the pitiful sound of a small girl sobbing.

The sun was rising in the east as four figures rested atop a hillside in Ancient Israel. The King of Israel had bragged about how Megiddo would be an impenetrable fortress, and I could see why he thought that way. The

Child of Light

location was perfect. It was hard to reach and had a commanding view of the surrounding area.

I turned to Lucifer. He was standing very quietly, clearly struggling with something inside of himself. "What's wrong?"

For a moment he remained silent, the only conversation happening inside his head, then he said, "There's something about this landscape." He gestured out to the valley below and the rising hills on either side. "Something... final." He shrugged. "It gives me the willies." He stretched his arms above his head and rotated his neck. "Let's see how the others are doing."

We walked over to our companions: the giant construct Gog and one half of the Potency in the form of a little girl, again with green hair and eyes. The two of them were knelt by the mud-brick wall of a deserted house. The baffled construct was peering at his hands, which he had held out, palms forward, in front of him.

"That's right," the strange little girl nodded. "Like that. Now, you pat them together like this." She proceeded to pat first one of her palms, then the other against the golem's giant paws. "Now it's your turn."

Gog knitted his brow and bunched up his lips in concentration. He just pounded his hands together three times, causing a resounding echo in the confined space. He grinned at the small girl, who sighed. "I don't think he's very good at it."

Lucifer hunkered down next to her and held out his arms. She sprung immediately into his embrace and snuggled her head into his shoulder. "He'll be better at other things," the seraph reassured her.

"I miss my sister."

"I know."

"When will I see her again?"

"I think you probably already know that. You're part of your mummy, remember, and she can see just about everything that has and will happen."

The small girl nodded disconsolately against the black material of the seraph's denim jacket. "It's going to be such a long time. What shall I do while I wait?"

"I think, perhaps, you should take a nap. A long one, to make sure you're refreshed."

"When I wake up, you'll come and play with me."

"I hope so."

A small smile touched her lips. "It wasn't a question. I know you'll come. You'll find me, hold me up for all to see, wrapped in your big claws..." She yawned. "We shall have so... much... fun..." Her green eyes slipped under her drooping eyelids and she fell asleep. As her body relaxed, it glowed a bright green and began to shrink in size, until it was just a hemispherical green stone, about the size of a human fist.

Lucifer smiled down with true affection.

"What did she mean about your *big claws*?" I asked.

Ignoring the question, the seraph turned to Gog. "Well, I have a very important job for you now."

In a short while, we had clambered through the deserted village, until Lucifer had found what he considered to be a suitable place. It appeared to be the lowest level of the abandoned settlement. Nodding to himself, he stretched out his hand and blasted fireball after fireball down onto the solid rock until, eventually, he had created an aperture which led through to a natural cavern below. We ventured in and the seraph looked around. Giving another nod, he blasted time and time again, fireball after fireball, creating a gently sloping passageway which he opened out into another cave. As I walked behind him, I noted how the blasted rock walls had the appearance of glass due to the impact of the intense heat.

Lucifer held up a hand. "I'd wait back there for a bit if I were you."

I withdrew a few metres and stood with the impassive Gog as the angel walked round and round the small cave blasting time and time again at the floor until he had fashioned it in such a manner that a small stone altar stood proud in the centre of the room. He nodded for the final time and placed the hemispherical potency on the surface of the natural stone table, affectionately rubbing its green surface with his thumb. Then, turning to Gog, he said, "I entrust her into your keeping. No one is to take her from this place except for me. Do you understand? If anyone happens to wander down here, you use that on them." The angel pointed to a huge scimitar that hung from the construct's belt. He had acquired it from somewhere during our stay. I wasn't sure that I wanted to know how or from whom...

The construct nodded his huge head in silent acceptance of the task, his enormous fingers gripping the hilt of the curved sword.

Lucifer smiled. "Thank you, friend. I'll make it worth your while when I return, but I'm afraid it will probably be a long, long time from now."

The construct huffed in acknowledgement and stood at the entrance to the small underground cavern, his wide arms crossed across his trunk-like chest. Lucifer patted him on the shoulder and then, taking me by the arm, guided me back up to the surface. When we reached the light of day, he concentrated his energy on the floor beneath us. I watched fascinated as the ground liquified under the pressure of the supernatural heat and he guided it vertically over the entrance to the passage that he had formed in the rock. When he had completely filled in the opening, he placed a hand on the now solid rock face and steam rose from beneath his fingers. As he withdrew his hand, I saw that a small emblem had been imprinted into the surface: a chalice in front of a sword with rays of light emanating outwards.

"I think it's going to be a long, long time for me until I return. This will help me find them."

I stared at the icons on the wall and swallowed. They reminded me of the chalice and the sword that the fiery Titan had held as it had destroyed the universe. "What are they?" I asked.

"They are the Cup and the Blade," came a youthful melodious voice from over my shoulder.

"They are Eternals," came an older version of the same voice.

"When they reunite, all will end," hissed the final, elderly voice.

"I was wondering when you would show your face," Lucifer snapped. "This is hardly the Indus Valley, is it? So much for providing me with answers. You've just sent us on a wild goose chase."

The young version of the Abyss turned its head from the ranting seraph and the middle-aged version lay its eyes firmly on me before the crone smiled to herself.

Lucifer couldn't fail to miss the implication. "What are you really up to? What is it with the boy?" He clenched his fist and it burst into flame. Taking a step forward, he rose the fist above his shoulder, preparing to strike.

The Abyss smiled, shook her head, and everything

changed.

Chapter Five

The first thing that struck me after the Abyss had transported us to the next stop on her magical mystery tour was the harsh change in temperature. I swore loudly as my body protested in shock at a rapid decline from the heat of Ancient Israel to the temperature of wherever it was that she had dumped us. The next thing was the poor quality of the air. As I stood in what appeared to be a small, refuse-filled, back alley, shivering through my grey hoodie, I grimaced at the taste of soot in my mouth.

"Where are we?" I asked.

Lucifer turned his head this way and that around the alley. He stopped in surprise when he realised that we had not travelled from Ancient Israel on our own.

"Decided to come and enjoy our suffering?" he snapped at the personification of the Abyss. "Watching from afar not providing you enough entertainment?"

"You misunderstand…" began the child.

"…our intentions," finished the woman.

"And what would they be?"

"Tell me Light," asked the crone, her wizened face half-obscured by the shadows of the alleyway, "if you

Child of Light

knew that someone wanted you dead. What would you do?"

"What sort of damn fool question is that? I'd do like anyone else would. Stop them."

The child nodded. "As I know you will."

The woman smiled slyly. "When the time comes."

"So, is it strange that I would do likewise?" asked the crone.

Lucifer frowned and genuine confusion replaced his anger. "Who the hell would want you dead? You stand as a barrier between the three Realms. Without you, Heaven, Beyond and the Physical Realm would…" He vaguely waved his hands in front of him, apparently lost for a description of such a cataclysmic occurrence.

"Then I saw a new Heaven and a new Earth," said the child.

"The first Heaven and the first Earth had disappeared," said the woman.

"And there was no more Sea," said the crone.

The three in one were silent, their body gently shifting from one form to the other as the seraph appeared to mull over these words. "So what do you want of us?" he eventually asked. "I mean, sure we've had a jolly old time of Ancient History 101, but there must be a purpose to your jumping us around willy-nilly."

"You are doing what needs to be done," said the child.

"You are seeing what needs to be seen," said the woman.

"You have one more task to perform," stated the crone.

"And then you'll send us back?"

The Abyss turned to face me and nodded before

she vanished.

Lucifer sighed and looked around the alleyway as if seeing it for the first time. "I suppose we'd better get on with this, then," he grumbled. "Have to be careful though. Victorian England was not known for being very accepting of strangers."

"You think that's where we are?"

My companion nodded. "Definitely." Then, smacking his lips together, he grinned, "It tastes just how I imagined it would from your school history books: of soot, horse shit and despair."

"Should I throw a protective bubble around us?"

He frowned as he looked me up and down. "I think you'll be okay. Your hoodie is grey and nondescript. You shouldn't stand out too much. As for my attire..." He snapped his fingers and the denim jacket and jeans transformed into a sharp black suit. "You like?"

I grinned. "Very dapper. How do you do that?"

"Angels are beings of energy, not matter. We can appear as we like. Talking of which..." He tapped his lapel and his two badges materialised, fastened to the fabric: the CND one and the Prefect one. "Okay, let's see exactly where we are."

We wandered out of the alleyway and straight into what appeared to be a busy thoroughfare. The local citizens all seemed to be in an incredible hurry to reach wherever it was that they were heading. Men in rough clothing hauled handcarts along cobbled streets; horse-drawn cabs clattered up and down, their passengers obscured from the outside world; barefooted children ran after each other, shouting with excitement.

I glanced at my companion and couldn't fail to notice the smile on his face and the slight flickering of amused flame behind his dark glasses.

"You like it here, don't you?"

"Victorian England or the Physical Realm in general?"

"I'm not sure. I'm guessing both."

"You'd be correct," he nodded, picking up an apple from a street vendor and tossing the woman a silver coin in exchange. The woman's eyes lit up at what was obviously an over-generous payment for a single piece of fruit. "Humanity is an incredible organism: so versatile; so able to adapt," he said between loud crunches. "When I watched it from the Presence, I couldn't quite comprehend how it managed to be so different to the angels. But, as I spent time inside you, the reason gradually dawned on me.

"It's their mortality.

"Angels are, by nature of their makeup, immortal beings. It takes a hell of a lot to snuff one out, and even if you're successful, they don't really die. They end up Beyond."

"You've mentioned that place once before. What is it?"

Lucifer paused on a street corner as the hustle and bustle of the town passed us by. He appeared to sigh, his shoulders rising and falling. "I guess it's fair to say it is probably the worst place in existence. When God created the Universe, first came Heaven. It was the realm of the spirit; a place of pure energy; the Eternal Realm. In it dwelt the angels. However, there was a by-product, as such; a place where God was *not*. This was Beyond, a hellish place where the rules of existence do not apply. Only the Abyss separated first the two Realms, then the *three* Realms when God later created this one in which we are currently freezing our backsides off. It is said that Beyond is where angels go should they," he wrapped the following word in finger quotes, "die. It is a place of punishment for us. However, as no angel, as far as I'm aware, has ever kicked the immortal bucket, Beyond just sits there, looming like a great existential elephant in the room."

"Could humans ever go there?"

"What? Like, on a day trip to the beach?" he grinned. "To be frank, I really don't know. I guess it would take a hell of a whack to accomplish something so monumental. Besides, unlike angels, humans believe that, one fateful day, all," he finished his apple, core and all, then waved his hand around the smoke, filth and noise that encompassed us, "*this* will end for them and they will move on to something else entirely. As a result, they scurry around doing what they can to enjoy their short time here."

Lucifer paused and looked at me from behind his dark glasses as I shifted uncomfortably from foot to foot.

"What is it?" he asked.

"I'm not one of them, am I?"

"What makes you say that?"

"When we were in Egypt, one of the constructs stabbed me. But, the wound healed almost instantly. I can't be human."

"Interesting. You're certainly not an angel, though. If you were, I would know. Half and half, perhaps?" he mused. "That in itself has certain implications."

I dodged around a young boy chasing after a mangy, one-eared dog. "Such as?"

"When we were in Egypt and you saw Eloise, your mother, what did you make of her?"

Child of Light

"She was scared, lost."

"What about her physicality?"

I thought back and recalled the young woman scared and lost in an ancient world, a pair of babies starting to grow inside her. "Nothing odd," I shrugged.

"Exactly!" The seraph pointed enthusiastically at the air in front of him. "She was human."

"So?"

"Well, the last time that I crossed her path, she was an Angeloi, an angel. In fact, she served me as I attended to my duties in the Presence."

"Oh! What do you think happened to her?"

"Not got the foggiest. My guess is that, whatever it was, took place after my sudden departure."

We walked on a little bit in thoughtful silence until I asked, "Who was Abaddon?"

The air immediately around us turned even more frosty than the winter morning. "He was an Angeloi, like your mother. We clashed over certain matters."

"Such as?"

"The Eternals, mainly." Lucifer grimaced. "Although there may have been another matter at the heart of it."

"My mother?"

"Your mother."

"When we saw that vision of the Indus Valley, it was quite apparent that you were my father yet, in Egypt, it was Abaddon's genetics that I felt inside of her."

The seraph just gave me a stony silence.

"What do you make of it?"

"I don't know. And that worries me." He paused as we rounded a corner, his eyes gazing up into the sky above a marketplace where vendors were setting up for a day's business. "Now, will you just look at that?"

My eyes followed his and my mouth ran dry as my stomach lurched inside of me. There before us was the spire of the church that the Abyss had shown me.

"No!" I shouted, turning to retreat in the opposite direction. "We have to get out of here."

A firm hand grasped my arm. "Alec? What's wrong?"

"I... I can't go there. I can't!"

A pair of dark eyebrows knotted behind a pair of black-lensed glasses. "Why ever not? You're scared to death, lad."

"She said that I would die there. She said that it's the lair of Kanor!"

"Who? Who said that?"

"The Abyss!" I screamed, oblivious to the stares my outburst was drawing from the market traders. "She came to me in Israel and showed me that church. She said that if I went there I would die!"

Lucifer swore under his breath. "Okay, right, let's look at this, shall we? Rationally. First, Kanor will not exist here until everything has gone to pot. Correct? The Divergence has to happen first. Do you see any constructs wandering the streets right now?"

I shook my head.

"Second, do you know who the most powerful person on this planet is right now? Me. That's who. Do you think for one second that I would let anything happen to you?"

Again, I shook my head.

"Good. Finally, why do you think we're here? Do you really think it's a random chance that she dropped us somewhere connected to Kanor? Or perhaps you think she thought we might want to buy a local delicacy from the market here?"

I stared up at the gothic spire that reached up into the sky then nodded in agreement with his logic.

"Good lad. Let's go and inspect this place of doom for ourselves, shall we?"

"All Saints: Parish Church of Wellington," as the hand-painted sign outside the main porch proclaimed, was unlocked. I had considered this to be odd, reckoning that surely they would not want it left unsecured, inviting theft or vandalism. However, as we quietly entered the ruined church, it was quite apparent that there was very little more damage that the poor building could suffer. Not only were most of the wooden pews scattered around the nave like discarded driftwood, but there was a huge, gaping hole in the ceiling. The stone floor felt wet beneath our feet and there was, rather bizarrely, a distinct smell of the ocean permeating the devastated edifice.

"I think the Mother's Union will have quite the job on their hands when they come to clean this weekend," Lucifer quipped as he edged his way around the debris to the centre of the nave. His eyes followed the path of destruction from the rood screen, where a life-size figure of Jesus hung on a cross, to the back of the church. He pointed to the broken, wet floor. "Whatever happened here, originated from that point. Something wet and forceful seems to have burst out of the floor. Any suggestions?"

"You don't think…?"

"Why else would she bring us here?"

I joined him in the centre of the church and together we made our way to the rear of the nave. As we did so, there was the unmistakable feeling that we were not alone. Just at the periphery of my hearing, I could make out a delicate sound of waves breaking upon a shore.

"You hear that?"

The seraph nodded. He knelt down at what looked like point zero for the origin of the church's destruction and placed his hand on the damp earth beneath the broken stones. His hand flared bright with flame and I was aware of other noises fighting to be heard. There was the sound of shouting; two voices arguing. Steel clashed with steel and a ferocious roar filled the air.

Lucifer pulled back and stood up. He nodded to himself.

"Let's go and pay the local clergy a visit, shall we? Perhaps they might be in need of our help?"

The vicarage was a large Georgian affair situated behind the church. We let ourselves into the house's grounds through an arched wooden gate that opened onto a sprawling driveway. Gravel crunched under our feet as we approached the imposing building.

"It looks big enough for five families," I commented.

Lucifer gave a small shrug and rapped on the solid door with his knuckles.

Momentarily, we were aware of the sound of someone hurrying up to the other side of the door. The large brass doorknob turned and the door creaked inwards. Standing on the threshold was a girl who was possibly a few years older than me, but it was incredibly hard to know for sure due to her wretched state. She was stick-thin and her skin was sickly pale. Her dark hair was pinned up under a maid's hat and her black uniform hung off her delicate frame. Her bright blue eyes seemed to lose focus as she opened her mouth to greet us and it looked as if she were about to faint. Lucifer stepped forwards and placed a steadying hand on her shoulder. "Are you okay, my dear?" he enquired, obvious concern in his voice.

The maid seemed to recover herself at the sound of the words and nodded. Her eyes scanned the pair of us in confusion.

"I see that your beautiful edifice is in need of repairs," Lucifer smiled reassuringly. "I thought that perhaps I might be able to help."

"Oh." The girl's voice was quiet and rather frail, as if it were unaccustomed to being used. "Vicar and his wife are just taking breakfast at the moment. I'm not sure as to whether they would want to be disturbed right now."

"What is the matter, Esther?" A primly dressed middle-aged woman appeared out of nowhere behind the flustered maid. "Who are these people?"

I decided there and then that I really didn't like the Lady of the House.

Lucifer just smiled and turned on the charm as he explained again that we were there to assist in the repairs of the church. We were travellers who had stopped off in this fine parish and felt that our incredible wealth would be suited to restoring the magnificent building to its original beauty.

Well, at the mention of the word *wealth,* we found ourselves ushered straight into the vicar's study and seated in a pair of nice chairs with cups of tea that had been poured into the finest bone china. In front of us was possibly the largest desk that I had ever lain eyes upon. I guessed it was made from mahogany. With all the precisely positioned books, stationery and files, it screamed "bureaucrat" rather than "priest". Lying in the middle of the desk was a newspaper that had been folded to show the headline "Bare Lane Butcher Strikes Again!", underneath which was a sketched reproduction of a rather graphic crime scene. I grimaced and concentrated on sipping my tea.

The hushed sound of footsteps on the plush carpet whispered the arrival of the vicar. He was a tall middle-aged man of approximately the same number of years as his wife. He was mostly bald with a faint line of white hair circumferencing his head. He wore a long, black cassock with an old-fashioned cloth dog collar. A pair of steel-rimmed spectacles sat perched upon a hawk-like nose and it was through these that he inspected us as he seated himself behind his desk.

Not once did he make an effort to welcome his guests or shake their hands.

"I believe that you are interested in our current renovation works," he said, his voice dry, clipped and precise. His grey eyes lanced through the spectacles with obvious mistrust.

Lucifer continued with his charm offensive. "Absolutely! My ward and I were passing through your gorgeous little town on our grand voyage and we were struck by the intrinsic beauty of the glorious edifice whilst being aghast at its current condition. May I inquire as to what befell the poor building?"

The cleric waved his hand almost dismissively. "There was a storm. The damage has been, as I am sure you have seen, quite extensive." He leaned back in his chair and pinched the bridge of his nose with his fingertips. "Quite frankly, any help that you could offer would be most welcome as the diocese has washed its hands of the whole affair."

Lucifer sat demurely, his hands clasped in his lap.

"My word, that's dreadful."

The vicar nodded. "They sent their representatives a few weeks back and can you guess what they said?"

"I couldn't begin to."

"*Naves are not our responsibility!*" the priest stormed, slamming his hand down on the surface of the desk, causing his papers to jump. "Naves are not our responsibility! I mean, what on earth are they thinking? Do they believe that I am made of money? The church has been shut since the disaster and the collection plates are now empty. They said that I should throw myself at the mercy of local businesses. Well, those local businesses do not know the meaning of the word *charity*. As soon as I approach them for aid, they turn their backs and shut their doors. What do they think I am? Some sort of gin-sodden beggar from the gutter? Do they think I am a whore that flashes her leg on a street corner"

The seraph and I exchanged looks as the vicar composed himself.

Lucifer settled his china cup on its saucer and smiled disarmingly at the cleric. "It really is a sorry state of affairs, these times, don't you think?"

The vicar narrowed his eyes and peered through his steel-rimmed spectacles. "What exactly do you mean?"

"Well, people just don't hold the church in the high esteem that they used to. They don't see how much it does for them, especially here at the parish level."

The vicar leant back in his expensive office chair and grunted in acknowledgement.

"It's all change, change, change, isn't it?" my companion continued thoughtfully.

"And none of it for the better," the vicar grumbled.

Lucifer sipped from his tea before resuming his apparent train of thought. "So many people trying to rise above their station. The middle classes wanting titles; the workers wanting their own houses; the filth thinking that the workhouse is too good for them…"

I started at that point, my jaw beginning to drop in horror at Lucifer saying such terrible things, but one word appeared in my head.

Wait.

So, I did.

"It wasn't like that when I was a young boy." The vicar was now staring out of the window of his study, out into the garden. "Everyone did as was expected of them, rich and poor alike. There was none of this social…" He twisted his fingers around as he searched for the right word. "Prevaricating. Yes, that's it. Social prevaricating. Once upon a time, everyone just got on and did what was expected of them. Now, they run around willy-nilly like headless chickens. Everyone is far too concerned with *bettering themselves*." His face twisted into a feral snarl as he said the words. "There's no order, no firm decision. No one to take matters into their own hands and just get things *done*."

"Rather like," Lucifer gesticulated to the newspaper on the desk, "that chap."

The vicar's attention snapped back into the room and he peered down the length of his nose at the top article in his newspaper. "Ah, the Butcher. I take it you're familiar with the case?"

Lucifer shook his head. "Sadly, no. My ward and I have been out of the country. It does look a grisly state of affairs."

The vicar shrugged. "Some stupid whores have

Child of Light

gone and gotten themselves gutted, up in a backwater seaside town. If they'd stayed at home and kept house properly for hard-working men, they would still be alive."

My stomach lurched in contempt at the supposed man of God's callous dismissal of the victims.

Lucifer just stared at the vicar without any trace of emotion and said, "A comment on the times, I am sure." He glanced at a mantle clock that ticked softly on a bookcase behind the priest. "Well, I think that it is about time that my ward and I were off rattling the tin can and getting the good and glorious of your fair town to give generously to the building fund."

The vicar picked up his newspaper and, with cold eyes, regarded the picture of the brutally murdered woman. "I would wish you luck, but I would just be wasting my breath."

"Well," Lucifer reassured him as we rose to leave, "I am sure that luck will not be necessary. My ward and I can be most persuasive."

We bade the horrid man a farewell and it was only as we exited the study that we noticed the maid, Esther, had been silently standing at the back of the room listening to our conversation.

On our visits to the local great and good of the town of Wellington, it soon became apparent that the vicar of All Saints was not exactly held in high regard. Every local businessman or dignitary with potentially deep pockets that we visited initially met our requests for funds with scorn and derision.

The most explosive of which was our first port of call, the local mayor, a certain red-faced man by the name of Cuthbert Richmond. "Hells bells!" the portly gent proclaimed as he stabbed at some offensive logs in his enormous fireplace. "If that wretched cleric was aflame, I wouldn't let my hounds urinate on him!" One of the said hounds whimpered in fear and scurried away from the hearth as Richmond swung around, still brandishing the flaming hot poker with which he gesticulated freely as he continued his rant. "Wellington born and bred, I am. Born and bred, I tell you. Not like that pale-faced cadaver. No! He swoops in, gaining himself a cosy little benefice from where he can preach his venom and merciless bile. Him and that she-devil of his. The pair of them, completely holier-than-thou, always looking down their noses at the rest of us whilst we work damn hard to build this town up from the dirt. Up from the dirt, I say! Pah!" He threw the poker into the fireplace and it clattered resoundingly against the grate. "Let him pay for the work from his own damn pocket. If he can't, then let him scurry off to preach to the poor foreigners over in Africa somewhere. We don't want him, that's for sure. If he goes then the bishop will do the place up good and proper before getting someone far more satisfactory." He paused. "Not that I'll be here to see them, mind."

"And why would that be?" Lucifer asked.

"I've had enough of all these parochial politics. I'm packing up and leaving. Already made a bid on a stately place out in Oxfordshire." The mayor's face softened a bit. "Lovely gardens. Even got some peacocks. No. Let the *vicar*," there was utter spite in the clerical title, "drown in his own piety. You'll not get any help from anyone in town."

"Oh, I beg to differ," Lucifer smiled over steepled fingers. "Especially when you've heard what my young ward has to say."

Child of Light

The look of confusion on the mayor's face almost matched that on mine.

"Go on, Alec," my companion smiled. "Tell the good mayor, here, that he *really* wants to start the barrel of donations rolling."

"Seriously?" Richmond laughed, thrusting his thumbs in the pockets of his tweed waistcoat. "You expect this young boy to persuade me? Well, it should be good for a laugh. Go on, lad," he beamed as he faced me. "Do your best!"

I turned to Lucifer for help but was just presented with an eyebrow rising in amusement from behind a dark lens. Swallowing down the rising panic, I looked at the imposing bulk of Cuthbert Richmond, his massive form silhouetted against the roaring fire. More precisely, though, I concentrated on his face, framed in a forest of ginger whiskers.

"Well, lad? What is it you have to say?"

Ignoring the jibe, I went behind the face. I pushed into the person behind the mask, one who was running away from town life because he was sick of all the backbiting and sharpened knives of local politics. I saw the man who wanted to raise a family in a place where his children could roam the streets safely at night and have room to play on large grounds that were surrounded by fields and cows. He really liked cows. And sheep. Such peaceful creatures that knew what they wanted and just got on with life. Not complicated at all. Simple minds for simple lives. That was what he wanted; what he longed for.

I took that hope, that desire, cradled it in my hands and stroked it, petted it. I soothed the raw emotions that attacked it, that caused the fear it could not be achieved and I released it in the luxurious meadow inside Richmond's mind.

Then, as the giant of a man sank slack-jawed into an overstuffed wingback chair, I pushed into the arms of his hopes and desires the notion that he should leave something behind for which he would be remembered. An enormously benevolent act of charity would be his parting gift for those citizens of this town that he served in his capacity as mayor.

"I think you'd really like to fund the renovations to the church," I stated with quiet firmness.

The man swallowed, blinked, closed his mouth and shook his head.

Turning to Lucifer, he inquired, "How much money would you like?"

And so it was that the wealthier citizens of Wellington each travelled along their own charitable road to Damascus. Local nobility gave generously of their bank accounts; builders and carpenters provided their time at reduced rates. Where there were solid brick walls of open hostility and animosity, I chiselled away with my burgeoning powers at the mortar that bound fast their air of reluctance until the great and good of the small market town in the East Midlands of England willingly did what they now perceived to be *the right thing*.

Within three days, an army of scaffolders had encompassed the church within and without in a lattice of woodwork and steel poles that was now akin to a hive swarming with worker bees. I don't think any such building project of its time was so completely overwhelmed with manpower. The sound of roofers singing and calling out to each other could be heard from the other side of the

Child of Light

market along with the pounding of the stonemasons' mallets and the carpenters' hammers. The inside of All Saints now smelt of freshly carved wood rather than stagnant damp as newly fashioned pews began to take shape. This pleasing aroma mingled with the rich tang of cement as the flooring was replaced, the master of the project berating his apprentices for the slightest mistake.

"You get that right, young Makinson!" I heard the dust-covered workman call out one time. "Make sure it's level. This is a house of God, not some cheap little brothel on Sheep Street frequented by that wastrel brother of yours!"

The young apprentice muttered quietly under his breath as he made a show of slapping an extra trowel of mortar around the flagstone he was setting at the west end of the church, his mind resonating with images showing quite clearly that he would, in reality, rather be off accompanying his sibling in the other aforementioned type of premises.

My abilities were something that I worked on whilst we stayed in Wellington. Lucifer suggested that it would be a good idea. He surmised that we were under no threat there, so it would be a suitable time to strengthen some whilst reining in others. The one that I really worked the hardest on was my reading of thoughts. Or, more precisely, preventing other people's thoughts from drowning me in a sea of overwhelming noise. Whilst my companion took it upon himself to be the foreman of the works, managing every facet of renovation so that the project ran like a well-oiled, turbocharged machine, I took to going for long walks around the town.

At first, I continued to find the constant mutterings in my head a distraction, an annoyance. However, I started to tell myself that they were not life-threatening. An angry vampire in Egypt was dangerous; a spurned fallen angel in Israel was a threat to my well-being. The odd glimpse of someone wishing their employer would jump in a cesspit or the image of a market trader being mentally undressed by a bored housewife were certainly distracting, but not ultimately fatal.

I thought back to my time in the far past when I had pictured the voices as a swarm of angry wasps trapped under a heavy blanket. It had worked incredibly well, staying put for my time in both Egypt and Israel, not slipping once. I found that odd. Surely a new skill like that should take practice? Yet the noises of others' minds had been a controllable dull whisper during all our time in the past. What was the difference here? Why were they edging out from under the blanket that I had thrown over them? Was it tiredness on my part? Perhaps it was the lack of personal peril? This seemed to me to be the most likely candidate. What with vampires, constructs and fallen angels, in Egypt and Israel there had been that constant feeling of fight or flight (probably with an emphasis on the latter). My subconscious must have been too busy working on exit strategies to worry about a passing bureaucrat counting up tax revenue for the previous quarter in his head as he walked down the road.

So, as I wandered around the Victorian streets, I tried to train my brain to consider different types of diversions and, to an extent, it worked. As I thought about how many cornflakes might fit in a bowl of cereal or how many steps it used to take me to walk to school, the noise of other people subsided back down, going once more from a roar to a hum.

The thing which really did diminish the sound

Child of Light

though was one thought in particular. Somewhere in the present day, there was a construct out and about looking for me: the one who had posed as my father. That creature of clay who had wandered every day into our kitchen, ruffled my hair and called me, "Champ!" was still out there. What was he planning? Would he track me down? What would he do if he found me?

Yeah. When I started to dwell on that, all sounds of others' banal thoughts evaporated from the puddle of my mind. The fear was overwhelming.

I decided to test my theory even more.

Lucifer and I had taken lodgings at the Golden Hart Hotel about a quarter of a mile away from All Saints. It was one of the oldest buildings in the town and one evening, whilst we were resting in front of a roaring fire in the communal room by the bar, the hotelier took great pride in informing us that Oliver Cromwell had rested there no less, brutally raping and murdering a serving wench during his stay before making his escape down a set of mythical tunnels that linked the hotel to a manor house on the other side of town.

Deciding that I didn't need my head filled full of urban myths and legends about dictators who had probably never even looked at the location of Wellington on a map, I made my excuses and headed out into the cold night, leaving the seraph working his way through a pack of Lucky Strikes while he exchanged ghost stories with the hotelier.

I walked away from the more civilised parts of town to an area where the streets became alleys and the gaslights became nonexistent. Drunks slept in doorways; prostitutes stood on street corners. It was definitely not the part of town where you would take your grandmother for a pleasant stroll. As I ventured further into darkening alleyways, I felt my heart begin to pound as the adrenalin production in my body went into overtime. The sounds of strangers' thoughts started to ebb into wispy background noise. They were there, just nowhere near as prominent. My senses were far more concerned with shadows that might or might not be lurking muggers and sounds that could possibly be the sliding of a knife being drawn from its sheath.

Satisfied that my little experiment had been a success and rather concerned that I might run into trouble, I circled back around on myself.

It was then that I became aware that I was being followed.

It wasn't the sound of a footstep that gave it away, nor an idle cough or muffled noise of a weapon being drawn. In fact, there was no external sound whatsoever. In my head, a presence had become apparent, one that was different to all the others that surrounded me in the dark, imposing terraced slum houses.

As I continued to walk, I pushed out with my senses and studied the presence, first viewing it from afar and then drawing in closer until I was inside it, looking out. I could actually see myself walking ahead of me.

It was at that point that the being swore and my feet suddenly parted company with the floor as I realised what the creature was.

A vampire.

I gasped for air as the creature ran with me in its grip to a dark, secluded dead end. It pushed me up against the wall and I could just about make out its features in the pale light of the moon. It was male, blonde and incredibly tall. Its eyes were almost directly in front of mine as it studied me.

"What are you?" it demanded in a deeply accented voice.

Then it sank its teeth into my neck.

Ignoring the pain, I reached out with my mind and touched his, searching for something that I could use as a weapon. A glimmer from its subconscious caught my attention and I focussed on it, drawing it to the present moment. The vampire retracted his teeth from my neck as he began to scream in terror, batting at unseen flames on his arm. I sank to the filthy floor, my hand shooting up to my neck as my skin sealed itself shut.

I may have taken a few seconds of glee just watching an immortal being with super strength chasing around a squalid back alley flapping its arms in an attempt to extinguish imaginary flames.

You have to enjoy the small pleasures in life.

Eventually, I became somewhat bored, so I waved my hand and the vampire stared dumbfounded at his sleeve. I reached out and touched his mind once more. His eyes snapped over to me as I said, "I believe your name is Doulos. I don't like being bitten."

The vampire stood staring at me. As he did, he absentmindedly ran a fingertip over his teeth. I couldn't help but notice that it came away dark. He frowned, stared at my blood, then dabbed it on his tongue. He had the appearance of a child that has tasted honey for the first time. His mouth opened in shock and he kept staring from his fingertip to me. Cautiously, he approached me, his arm out in a non-threatening manner. I remained silent as he knelt down next to me and ran his hand over my neck.

"Not a mark," he whispered.

"I'm a quick healer."

He shook his head. "You're more than that. Far more." He bent his head low. "I am at your service."

Well, that hadn't been expected.

At that moment, there was a loud cracking noise and Lucifer walked into the alleyway. His dark glasses surveyed the situation and he gave a wry smile. "Am I disturbing something?"

"I honestly don't know," I shrugged.

Doulos stood and rounded on the seraph. He frowned and seemed to inhale.

Lucifer flexed his right hand and the fingers burst into flame.

The vampire's hands shot out in front of him. "No! No! I mean you no harm. I... I..." His head snapped back and forth between the two of us. "He," he said, pointing at me, "is one of the Twins and you…" he gesticulated to Lucifer. "You are…" He sank down onto one knee, his head staring at the dirt-packed floor. "You are my creator. Your blood runs through my veins."

Lucifer stroked his chin in thought with his flaming fingers. "I'm pretty sure I've never had the pleasure. I think I would remember."

"Would you, though?" I dragged myself up from the floor and walked over to my travelling companion. "You said yourself that your memory is somewhat patchy."

The seraph shrugged and then asked the vampire, "What exactly do you mean by *creator*?"

"You gave birth to the Children of Cain. It's said that part of you escaped a dreadful prison which was holding you and travelled through time with the one you loved. You took her to the Ancient Levant and turned Cain after he slew his brother Abel, infusing him with your angelic blood. It's that which I can smell on you. It is the purest

Child of Light

essence of every Child of Cain."

I watched Lucifer for any sort of reaction. This was a biggie, the notion that he had created this shadowy league of vampires. He just stood still like stone, the fire in his eyes glimmering thoughtfully in the dark behind his glasses. "Ring any bells?"

"None," he replied. Then, to the vampire: "Tell me, did I give you any instructions after this little biblical *snackfest*?"

Doulos nodded. "Find the Eternals; Protect the Twins; Await the Divergence. Those are the commands that you told us to pass on to every vampire that we should create. They are what my mother told me and..." he paused, "what I told my son." His eyes rose from studying the floor. "This boy is one of the Twins."

Lucifer shook his hand and the flames vanished. He crossed his arms and seemed to be weighing up the vampire's revelation. After a somewhat tense moment, he asked, "So, if my companion here is one of these *Twins*, what of it? What does that mean?"

Doulos frowned. "We are not sure. You never told us what they were for, just that we had to protect them." He turned to me. "So that is what I must do. You should come with me; meet the rest of us. We will decide what needs to be done next."

I looked frantically over to Lucifer who just groaned. "Not happening, friend. At least, not right now. We're just passing through and have other places to be."

"But your commands..." The vampire took a step forward.

"Alec, if you would be so kind?"

I reached out and touched the mind of the vampire. Inside him, I sensed a whirling ball of confusion, fear and regret. Through his mind's eye, I saw another man: tall, broad. Doulos held him in a shroud of love, concern and despair. I could not ignore the overwhelming paternal bond. I took this man and held him up on a pedestal — unmissable, central to the vampire's being. "You will forget that you saw us tonight," I said, leaning heavily into my words as the vampire flinched. "Instead, you will put your family in order. Now, turn around, walk away and remember nothing of us, except for what I have just told you."

The vampire stared for a brief moment as his subconscious wrestled with this paradox of not knowing that the people who stood in front of him existed before turning on his heel and walking out of the alley and out of our lives.

Lucifer let out a low whistle as he watched Doulos wander off into the night. "Impressive. You're really coming on. It makes me wonder how much you'll eventually be capable of."

"What do you make of what he said, about you creating the vampires?"

Lucifer's shoulders rose and fell as he sighed. "Another random thread of mystery in the ever-unravelling tapestry of life. I suggest we don't tug at it right now for fear of accidentally pulling everything apart. We wait until we have more information. One task at a time, okay?"

I nodded. It made sense.

He stretched and clicked the joints in his shoulders. "Anyway, the night is late and we'd better get back to the hotel. Busy day tomorrow."

"Why's that?"

He grinned, fire dancing behind his dark glasses, illuminating his face in the gloom of the alleyway. "In the morning, we're going to see a man about a font."

The stonemason's workshop was situated a few miles outside Wellington in a place called Irlingbury. A small hamlet with designs on the dizzying heights of village-hood, Irlingbury was quite literally a collection of cottages around a small square just off the main road that led away into the rolling countryside. At the far end of the settlement was a wooden fence with a gate that hung ajar. Letting ourselves in, Lucifer and I wandered through a bizarre assortment of roughly hewn stone and half-finished or discarded statuary. The objets d'art ranged from small gnome-like garden ornaments to massive stone pillars covered in intricately carved designs.

The seraph paused briefly at a set of four lifelike winged figurines and, clasping his hands behind his back, bent to study the faces of the angelic replicas.

As he did so, I was aware of talking and the door to a small wooden shed opened. A young woman exited. Upon catching sight of us, she thrust something into the pocket of her apron. Studiously avoiding my gaze, she hurried out of the yard, the gate slamming against its frame as she did so.

I noticed that Lucifer's attention had left the statuary and his eyes had followed the woman's hasty exit. He nodded to himself, straightened up and strode over to the small shed.

I followed behind.

The seraph was about to knock on the door when it swung inwards and there, in front of us, stood a rather grizzled man in his late forties. His hair was light grey — whether through age or dust, I could not tell. Deep lines framed his light brown eyes and fine stubble covered his chin. He wore a smock that was of a similar shade to his hair, and it was in the pockets of this that he thrust his hands as he asked, "How can I help you, gentlemen?"

"I was just admiring your work," Lucifer beamed. "Incredibly accurate detail."

"I just carve what I see," the man shrugged.

"Of that, I have no doubt," the seraph mused. "In fact, that's why we're here. We have a very special job that requires your undertaking. It will require your very special skills."

A smile formed on the man's mouth that was not matched by the look in his eye. "Thank you for the flattery, sir. I am just a humble stonemason, doing what any other member of my trade does."

Lucifer removed his glasses and the man's face turned white as he stared up at the angel's fiery pupils. "I think we both know that what I'm after requires more than just the accurate tappings of a mallet and a chisel. Perhaps we ought to talk inside your," he peered into the small shed, "*office*?"

The insides of the small wooden building were surprisingly spacious. It seemed that the stonemason was a stickler for order and keeping absolutely everything in its place. All his tools were hung up neatly on the wall and the work surfaces were clear of any clutter. There were two stools situated next to a small table. Lucifer seated himself on one and gestured for the man to take the other. Even without my gifts, it would have been easy to feel the nerves that were rolling off the poor craftsman. He visibly flinched as my companion said, "I believe that your name is Matthias. People in these parts speak very highly of you."

Child of Light

Matthias just nodded mutely, his eyes looking anywhere but at the burning balls of fire right in front of him.

"What was it you made for her?" Lucifer inclined his head to the door of the shed. "A love talisman? Something to guarantee that the local village stud would finally notice her?"

The stonemason shrugged and the hint of a smile touched the edge of his lips. "Isn't it always?"

Lucifer nodded in agreement. "It's a funny thing, magic. People always dismiss it, but when their backs are up against the wall and they have nowhere else to turn to, they always fall back on the old ways, don't they?"

"I only does what I do to help folk!" Matthias protested, finally staring Lucifer squarely in the face. "I never 'urt no one."

Lucifer reached out for his hand. The terrified man tried to snatch it away, but the seraph pulled it back, resting it on the table between them. "I know," he said, his hand gently rubbing the back of the stonemason's large paw. "I could tell that the moment that I walked into your yard."

Matthias frowned in confusion.

"It's the smell. Every type of magic has its own distinct odour. Dark, destructive magic smells sour. Only those who wish ill intent can bear to be around it. Yours... yours smells of peonies and roses that have been washed by a spring shower. It dances around my nose and, when I breathe it in, it skips across my palate. How long have you been practising?"

"Since I was a young 'un. Runs in the fam'ly. Like," he gestured to his tools, "the craft."

Lucifer nodded. "Along with the sight?"

Matthias nodded.

"Where do you go?"

"Some place I cannot fully comprehend. There are voices, so many voices and they all seem to me to be singing. Happy singing, you know? Praising and the like."

"Was that where you saw my four friends out there?"

The craftsman gave a non-committal shrug. "I *think* so. It's kind of hard to recall." He paused. "What is it that you want from me?"

Lucifer leaned back on his stool, removing his hand from that of the stonemason. "I take it that you are aware of the current works that are being undertaken at All Saints?"

"News travels. News of a curious pair of visitors who seem to have whipped the whole town up into a frenzy of activity. I take it that would be both of you?"

"You would be correct. The work is coming along nicely, however, the church is going to need one thing that the good folk of Wellington can't provide."

Matthias rubbed a dusty hand against his stubbled chin. "I heard that the font came off quite badly in the storm. A metal affair if I recall. Sat on a wooden table? Will they not just beat it back into shape?"

"I took a moment to inspect the damage yesterday. When they come to evaluate the font's..." Lucifer twirled his fingers as he searched for the correct word, "*feasibility*, I'm sure they will seek a replacement. They'll need something far more durable."

"You want me to fashion a new font then?"

"Oh, I want far more than that. I want you to make a prison."

A short while later and upon the workbench along

the side of the shed were lain out the tools of the stonemason's trade: five different-sized mallets, a measuring rule, a selection of chisels, chalk, a bowl containing incense and charcoal, a sprig of sweet-smelling flowers, a small black book of spells.

"What you're asking for is incredibly specific," he said as he picked up the small book and began thumbing through the well-read pages.

"The entity that's plaguing me is a very powerful creature," Lucifer growled. "Specifics will make sure that things go according to plan.

"*My* plan."

Matthias nodded. Slipping the book into his smock, he selected a medium-sized mallet and an incredibly sharp chisel. Nodding to the incense and the flowers, "If someone would be so kind?"

I stepped forward and picked up the items before we all headed out into the yard.

"I have a piece of stone that should be suitable. A gorgeous piece that I started polishing just the other day. It called to me," he explained. "Now I know why." He stopped at a dark grey block that came to about waist height. Its flecked patterns glinted in the winter sun. Placing his tools on the floor, he fished out his spell book. Selecting the correct page, he sat it on top of the stone. He motioned for me to place the bowl and the flowers on either side. "Thank you."

Using a long match, Matthias ignited the charcoal and the smell of sweet incense began to waft up into the air. The mason placed a finger on the open pages of the book and began to recite words in a convoluted language that I could not understand. When he had finished, he took the flowers and burnt them in the bowl with the incense. Green smoke began to drift up into the air and he nodded in satisfaction. Taking the bowl, he walked seven times around the block of stone before coming to rest in front of Lucifer. "You said that you want to be the key to this prison?"

The seraph nodded. "Only I must be able to open it."

Matthias nodded as a worried crease appeared on his brow.

"You need my blood, don't you?"

The stonemason nodded.

Lucifer flexed his fingers and a knife appeared in the grasp of his right hand. He sliced it across the open palm of his left and squeezed crimson liquid into the bowl.

"I need you to stir it now," Matthias explained. "Seven times, clockwise."

"It's always seven," Lucifer muttered as he did as he was instructed using the tip of his knife. "And now?"

"Please smear the paste on the stone. Horizontally. Near the top."

The seraph dipped his hands into the bowl and drew up a fair amount of the arcane mix. "Here?" he asked, his fingers poised by the stone.

"Straight across."

Lucifer pulled his fingers across the smooth face of the block, leaving a black smear on the grey surface. "Is that everything?"

"Almost. Sorry. If you don't mind?" He handed me the bowl and picked up his carving tools. "Prisons are a place of fear. As such, this needs to be engraved with the name of the person or thing that you fear the most."

Lucifer's eyebrows knotted behind his dark glasses. "Won't that look a tad odd in a church?"

"I can hide it," Matthias reassured him. "I could perhaps engrave it as a mnemonic? Put the letters of the name at the beginning of the words of a phrase?"

The fire in the seraph's eyes twinkled as he told the mason the name. "And the final part of my request?"

Matthias grimaced.

"I need her power. If I don't get it, my friend and I are stuck here."

"The incantation I used will draw some essence from the being that you imprison, but not much. You will be able to use its power once, but that is all."

Lucifer nodded. "It will have to do."

Matthias breathed a sigh of relief as he held his chisel in front of the stone and raised his mallet. "Now, what phrase would you like me to carve in order to hide that name you told me?"

The font was the last piece of ecclesiastical furniture to be reinstalled. It took a team of ten men, intricately guided by the fretting Matthias, the best part of a day to get it sited in exactly the right place. Lucifer stood with them, providing them with precise instructions as to left or right, backwards or forwards, until he finally gave an assured nod to the stonemason who then proceeded to cement the stone pedestal into place.

When it was done and the labourers had departed, Matthias approached us, his hands rubbing nervously against one another. "Is it to your satisfaction?"

Lucifer walked up to the stone font and reached out to touch the grey surface but, at the last moment, snatched back his hand, instead circling around the bowl, inspecting the man's handiwork. "It's perfection," he whispered, the bowl grasping his full attention. "You are incredibly skilled, my friend."

The humble mason shrugged. "I just does what I does."

"But you do it so well." Lucifer cocked his head to one side and I was aware of the soft sound of water eddying around my head. "I think, perhaps, you had better leave us now. There are certain things that you should not see."

The poor man muttered a nervous farewell and scurried off out of the church.

Lucifer stood in front of the font, his foot playing with a loose flagstone that a bored apprentice had not seen fit to cement properly into place. "You can come out now," he smiled.

The sound of rushing waves in my head crescendoed and the personification of the Abyss appeared directly behind the font. She circled the stone bowl, fluidly morphing through her three forms. Lucifer kept a clear distance from her, staying constantly on the opposite side of the font as she admired the handiwork. Pausing at the front of the bowl, she ran her young, then middle-aged, then elderly hand over the carved inscription. "Do you think you have won, Light?"

Lucifer regarded her from the westernmost part of the nave. "What do you mean?"

"Do you really think I would not know you have built a prison in which to incarcerate me?"

The seraph leant forward and placed his hands on the font. "Ah yes, the mighty, all-seeing Abyss. You see, there's something that I don't get."

"And what would that be?"

"You've seen that you will die. It is a concrete fact, more solid, more immovable than this very font.

Child of Light

"And yet you're trying to stop it."

Two of the most powerful entities in the universe glowered at each other inside a small church in a market town in Victorian England. I started to wonder if all the rebuilding work had been in vain.

Eventually, the Abyss broke the stand-off as three voices said as one, "We should all be in control of our own destiny."

Lucifer's lips turned up in a hard smile. "Exactly." His hands erupted in flame and the words on the front of the font became blindingly bright. I reflexively threw my hands up for protection as the light from the letters radiated out and enveloped the personification of the Abyss. Her three individual forms split apart and screamed as one as the beams of light wrapped around her as if they were physical cords or rope. The girl, the woman and the crone twisted and tugged at their bonds, their watery hair flowing out behind them, their fiery vestment burning bright. The eyes of the three seemed to expand wider than their faces and their mouths became cavernous holes. A thrumming noise seemed to be building up from within them. I saw Lucifer brace himself for an onslaught.

It came in the form of thousands of insects that erupted from the three open mouths of the Abyss. Fiery flying insects that resembled locusts surged out into the nave and enveloped the seraph. For a brief moment, he looked like a crazed apiarist at a country fair demonstrating how bees were our friends and made wonderful, living clothing. The locusts filled the church with their overwhelming drone as they suffocated and subdued the seraph. I stood helpless as the binding tethers around the Abyss began to fall slack.

I did the only thing that I could. I reached out and

touched the mind of the angel that had rebelled against God.

At first, there was just frustration and anger. The psyche of the sole member of the rank of Seraphim whirled and spun faster than any fairground ride designed to induce vomit-filled thrills as the locust-like creatures of the sentient ocean crawled over his skin. The power the angel's mind contained, should anyone ever attempt to harness it, could work wonders. I envisioned spreading my arms and I wrapped them around the screaming morass of primal chaos. I felt its crazed spinning untamed power respond to my touch, drawing energy from my own powers, and the onslaught of the Abyss responded by increasing tenfold. Both Lucifer and I cried out as she began to batter us with the greatest weapon that she possessed.

Her omniscience.

A dizzying array of images began to flood our heads, most of which struck us at such a high velocity that we were unable to discern what they actually were. They were like one of those air hockey pucks careening from side to side of the vibrating table as the player tries to find a chink in their opponent's rapid defence. I saw vague glimpses of Heaven, of Lucifer gazing up at the Eternals, of his shouting at another angel, of him walking down the white halls with my mother.

I felt a puck almost strike home and the image of my mother spiralled around in my head as I grimaced, desperate to hold on. I saw her wandering the Egyptian city we had visited in the dark of night. I saw her surrounded by numerous textbooks, frantically scribbling notes into an exercise book. I watched as she changed form into that of a dark-haired, bespectacled woman and walk unseen through crowds of people, hiding in plain sight and on a mission that she knew would take many, many years. I felt myself cradled in her arms as if I were a baby just a few minutes old. With me was Amanda, my sister, also freshly born into this physical world. Our father, the seraph whose powers I was trying to protect, and our mother, the woman that he loved, gazed down at us. The smiling blonde woman waved her fingers in front of us and we gurgled as pretty lights filled our minds. The dark-haired man touched our button noses and tiny flames danced on our soft skin. Then there was a crash and the door to the room our family moment burst inward. Construct after construct stormed into the room and there was blackness.

I shook my head and struggled to peer through half-open eyes at Lucifer. The locusts were undulating over his body, swarming up his chest and along his arms. He shook his head, but I felt it wasn't at the discomfort of the creatures. It was at something else. Something that he was seeing inside his own mind.

I reached out to touch what he saw.

I cried out as if I had touched a roaring hearth, my psychic powers slamming back in my face.

Lucifer bellowed and the locusts erupted into flame. My knees weakened and I slumped to the floor as the sight in front of me stole my breath and locked it away in a place that I could not find. Behind the newly installed font, hovering two metres above the stone floor, was a being of pure fire. Six enormous wings beat behind him, keeping him afloat, and a mask of rage burned on his face. The seraph grasped his hand into a fist and the cords around the Abyss tightened once more. He yanked at them and she flew across the church, powerless against his anger-fuelled intent. With his free hand, Lucifer reached out and seemingly snatched at the air in front of him. The three forms of the living river screeched in agony as they merged back into an undulating mass of one. As they did so, a pulse of water burst from their midst and spurted towards the seraph's awaiting grasp. A grin cracked open on the front of his fiery face as he intently studied the whirling ball of water before absorbing it into his fingers of flame. With a final pull, he yanked the Abyss to the font. She continued to scream as she plummeted into its bowl, filling it to the rim. Lucifer released the cords that bound her and dropped a fireball on top of her watery form. A mushroom cloud of steam billowed up and then... there was calm.

Then there was nothing. Just quiet.

Almost.

As I stepped closer to the font, I was sure that I could hear the quiet whispering of the sea, just as you do when you hold a seashell to your ear. "So, is that it?" I asked. "Is she trapped here? In this font?"

The fiery seraph drifted back down to the floor and resumed his normal form before waggling his hand back and forth. "Not exactly. Let's face it," he grinned, "she's a rather large entity. An ocean that surrounds the three Realms, remember. No. She was using this place as a gateway to the Physical Realm. I've just changed the locks on the door."

"And you're the key?"

He nodded. "Her physical form and creepy threefold manifestation won't be able to break through without me. People will still hear her song, though. It's part of Creation, after all. It resonates through everything. It will just be more of an itch."

Child of Light

"What if someone tries to scratch it?"

Lucifer stared darkly at the font, embers smouldering in his eyes.

"You took something from her. Just now. Before you imprisoned her. What was it?"

Lucifer studied the hand that had absorbed the water from the Abyss. "Some of her power, just as Matthias promised. Enough of her energy to get us home…"

"I'm sensing it was more than you expected."

He just nodded.

"When we were fighting her, I saw images of you and my mother. I think the Abyss was trying to distract me and break my bond with you."

Lucifer continued to stare at the font.

"What did she show you?"

For a moment, the seraph was broodily silent, his fingers just stroking his chin as the flames behind his dark glasses danced ponderously. Eventually, he said, "I think it was my future, but it may also have been my past. Something… inevitably cataclysmic."

I waited for him to elaborate. He didn't, so I asked, "Are we done?"

Lucifer raised an eyebrow in secretive amusement. "Almost."

The unveiling of the font and the recommissioning of the church was quite a grand affair. Socially, that was; not spiritually. The service was exactly what I expected from the local clergyman: perfunctory, dogmatic and dull. The hymns were kept to a minimum with the congregation mumbling along to a subdued organ for a maximum of three verses to each supposed song of praise and thanksgiving. Ritual was non-existent and I did my best to not look at my watch through the thirty-minute sermon on hell and damnation.

You would have thought that as the newly re-opened church was full to the rafters of Wellington's finest (and, indeed, wealthiest) he would have put on more of a show. But no, apparently he was for sticking to his liturgical and theological guns and blasting away any goodwill that Lucifer and I had built up for the church.

Lucifer, curiously, was somewhat distracted throughout the service. Every now and then, I caught him glancing to the back of the church where the vicar's deathly thin housemaid was seated. I have to admit that she drew my attention too, mainly because out of the whole congregation, hers was the one voice that sang clear and with real energy. Looking at her near-skeletal frame, I wouldn't have thought she had it in her.

"What is it?" I asked the seraph.

He shook his head. "I'm not sure. There's something about the girl. She's important."

"In what way?"

Lucifer made a curious little sucking noise with his lips and turned back to the front. "I don't know. When she first met us, there was something there. Something I can't quite put my finger on."

The service dragged on until people realised that it had actually finished. The general residents of Wellington filed out in a somewhat confused manner, obviously feeling that they had missed the point of it all. They left behind a select few of the donors to the repair works. The great and good of Wellington milled around at the back of the church, admiring the font as a reporter's cameraman set up his kit for a shot of the newly installed stonework.

The young maid made to leave with the congregation but Lucifer caught up with her and placed a gentle hand on her arm. "Please, my dear, stay."

Her bright blue eyes flashed nervously across the nave to her employer who was pontificating at great length to a small group of men, including a very bored Mayor Richmond. "I... I... do not feel it would be proper."

Lucifer smiled and cocked his head to one side. In a low voice, he said, "Oh, I disagree. I feel it would be most apt... all things considered."

The girl frowned. "Things, sir?"

"How might one put it? Let's just say I feel it could be useful for you to be in this photo for *future generations*." He led the embarrassed girl over to the group that was arranging itself in front of the camera and, ignoring her scowling employer, situated her comfortably in the shot.

Once the photo had been taken, Lucifer inclined his head to the door of the church and I quietly followed him. The last thing we heard as we stepped out of the church and into a blinding light was the voice of the cameraman commenting that the word *naves* was spelt with an "N", not a "K", followed by the wailing of the vicar.

Chapter Six

We were back in the small cabin. I opened my mouth to speak, but a rasping croak was all that came from my parched lips and taut larynx. The sound of a running tap reached my ears and Lucifer walked over with a glass of water. I took the drink and cherished every blissful drop of cold liquid.

"Take your time," he said, seating himself on the edge of the rickety bed. "You've been on quite a journey."

"Definitely. How long were we away?" I managed between soothing sips. I rotated my shoulders and felt the tendons creaking in protest. "It feels like I haven't moved in weeks."

"Not long. A few hours. Your body's just been paralysed for the duration. It'll take a while to recover properly. Spirit walks can do that if you're not used to them."

"Spirit walk? You mean we never actually left here?"

Lucifer waggled his hand back and forth in his non-committal manner. "Well, I say *spirit walk*, but that was just technically our little trip up to Heaven. No, we were physically transported down the timeline by our watery friend. We just happened to remain here as well."

I frowned. "I'm not sure I understand entirely."

"Unfortunately that comes as standard when dealing with uber-powerful entities." He paused as I winced at a spasming muscle in my neck. He reached out a hand and flames danced on his fingertips. "Here. I can help." The small flames sprung from his fingers and danced around the base of my neck, not once burning my skin or singeing my clothes. I felt my muscles and tendons warming under their slow movements and my body quickly unknotted.

"Thanks. That's much better." I shifted around and perched myself up on the side of the bed. "One question…"

Lucifer raised an eyebrow. "Just one?"

I chuckled. "Okay, one *current* question. What was it with getting the maid, Esther, in the photograph?"

"When I took on the power to travel through time for that final jump, some other residual power of the Abyss came with it. Just a small token of her infuriating omniscience. I instinctively knew that the photo was going to be important as will that young woman."

"Really?" I frowned. "To be perfectly honest, I don't think she actually has long left in this world, you know? Or should that be *had* long left?"

"You'd be surprised what bones Fate can throw you when you're a starving dog," he shrugged. "Now, her employer…" A wicked grin spread across his face as he momentarily closed his eyes, observing something that only he could see. "Well, sometimes people just get what they deserve."

"So, do you think you'll keep this power?"

He shook his head. "it's like a filter over reality. I can

see what's in front of me, but the filter is clarifying certain finer details that are going to happen later. Unfortunately, it's already starting to fade. The jump from the past must have used up most of the juice I purloined from our watery friend." He looked at me in a curious manner.

"What?"

"There is one thing, though. Something inside of you, from your near future. I can see it as it's starting to fade away. We need to get you somewhere safe. I can only do so much for you as I still need to remain hidden. When I look at you, I see someone else looking after you. In fact, I think it'll be a relationship of mutual protection for both of you."

"Can you see his name?"

I felt a gentle tickling inside my skull. "Sam Spallucci." Lucifer frowned as I started. "What is it?"

"I know that name. Abaddon mentioned it. He said that he'd met Spallucci and that I'd been with him."

"Time travel's a bitch," Lucifer grunted and the tickling sensation inside my head became a heavy pressure. "Damn it, it's fading more rapidly now. It's like I'm trying to hold a block of ice with fingers of fire. I'll grab what I can before it all melts away." His eyes flared behind his glasses and the sensation of pressure increased as his head cocked to one side in apparent amusement.

"What is it?"

"Well, he looks like quite an interesting character. I can't see *too* much in the way of detail but, apparently, he's going to get up to all sorts. Quite a crucial figure, one might say."

"Care to share?"

"Probably best I don't. Spoilers," he shrugged. "Oh!"

"What is it?"

"I… *know* him," the seraph murmured more to himself than to me. "Or rather, I've *met* him, too. Twice in fact. But I have no recollection of either event. Not got a clue as to how, either. As far as I was aware, I'd never left Heaven before jumping down into you."

I grimaced as something inside of me tugged sharply as he tried desperately to uncover more information.

"Sorry. One was on… a *beach*? I was so angry. Young too. The other… Oh!"

"What?"

"The church! All Saints! I first met him there. We shook hands…" Lucifer grimaced and I yelped in pain.

Then there was blessed relief as the connection broke.

"It's gone. Faded away now. Sorry about that."

I shrugged. "Did you find out where he is?"

My companion nodded. "Lancaster. He lives in Lancaster."

"Quite a journey."

The seraph nodded. "I can fill you in on things as we travel. Your Old Man can impart his wisdom upon you."

"So you definitely think you're my father? What about what I sensed in Egypt? What about Abaddon?"

"What *about* Mister Tragic Goth?" He crossed his arms and peered at me over his glasses. "What did the Abyss show you when we fought in the church?"

"I saw images of my mother. One of them was her and you together as she held Amanda and me in her arms. We were a family."

Lucifer nodded. "I saw that image too. It filled my

heart with such joy... We may not have got to the Indus Valley in person, but that image proves to me that I'm your father."

"Do you remember that actually happening?"

He shook his head. "Like I said, time travel's..."

"...a bitch."

The seraph smiled and placed a hand over mine, "But, I know what we saw and I know what I *feel*. You are my son and screw biology."

We both sat smiling on an old bed in a ramshackle cabin in the far reaches of the British Isles, quietly enjoying one of those perfect moments. The sort that poetry can never truly describe, that comes very rarely in a person's lifetime.

However, there was an annoying tickle at the back of my mind. Our familial moment hadn't been the *only* thing that Lucifer, my father, had seen. There had been something else. Something that had deeply troubled him. I made to press the matter again but was suddenly aware of a disturbance outside.

Our faces turned in unison towards the door of the cabin.

"Trouble," said Lucifer.

"Constructs," I confirmed.

"How many can you feel?"

I reached out past the walls of the cabin and let my senses spread out across the driveway and scrubland in front of the building. "Five. They're not alone. They have eight humans with them too." I concentrated and passed silently through the minds of each individual. "They're police. Some sort of SWAT team, armed. They're here for me. They've got an inspector of some sort. He's a construct and he's giving orders to surround the building.

He…" Something disturbingly familiar tickled my brain. "Oh!"

"What is it?"

I looked at the seraph. "It's the one that was posing as my father."

As a bullhorn-enhanced voice declared that the property was surrounded and that I was to give myself up peacefully, Lucifer and I discussed tactics.

"He looks different," I said as I utilised the eyes of the members of the armed unit to study the monster that had kept me a prisoner since birth. "When he was posing as my father, he was your typical office guy: nondescript, glasses, a forced smile to cover the years of regret spent in a pointless job."

Lucifer chuckled.

"Now…" I shook my head. "Now he's tall, somewhat gaunt. He looks shabby. But it feels like a front. He has absolute control over his force. They will do whatever it is that he asks of them.

"Including *open fire*?"

"That would be my guess."

The seraph stroked his chin in thought. "*My* guess is the construct infiltrated the police at your house when they investigated the fire. He most likely killed the officer in charge, took his place and labelled you as a murderer."

I groaned in frustration. "How do we get out of this? Even if I just throw up a protective bubble, they'll still be hunting me down. I'm a fugitive now."

Lucifer smiled.

It wasn't a reassuring smile.

"What have you got in mind?"

"I escaped Heaven by convincing everyone there

that I was dead.

"We do the same here."

The wooden door swung out into the cool, early morning sun. From the shadow of the cabin, I could see the glint of sunlight on gun barrels as they pointed at me from behind police vans and cars.

"Step out with your hands up," came the enhanced nasal voice of my former jailor. "Come out slowly."

I took a deep breath and braced myself.

Even if this worked, it would hurt like hell.

I formed an image in my mind, concentrated on forming every important detail and, as I ran out into the driveway, shoved it out into the minds of all those police surrounding the building.

Their eyes saw a gun in my hand.

Their ears heard multiple cracks of gunfire.

As I heard the sound of safeties being unsnapped and shoulder butts eased up against uniforms, I began to retreat backwards, down the side of the cabin. Towards the cliff edge behind it.

"Do not fire!" screamed the bullhorn. "Repeat, do not fire!"

Well, we couldn't be having that. It would ruin the plan.

I pushed again and screamed into the voices of the hesitant police officers, "Fire! Now! Take him down!"

And they did.

The sound of the repeating volleys was deafening but was quickly obliterated by the excruciating pain of bullets slamming into my chest. My backwards motion was accelerated by the velocity of the impacts. My right foot trod thin air and the surrounding land disappeared from view to be replaced with blue sky as a howling wind tore at my skin.

As I crashed into the waves down below, blood streaming from my gunshot wounds, one thought went through my head: *Sam Spallucci, whoever you are, this had better be worth it...*

A.S.Chambers

Author's Notes

Hello, kind reader, and thank you for buying and reading what has certainly been for me, at least, a true labour of love. I hope you enjoyed this dip into Alec's past that explores the curious teenager's relationship with the fallen seraph, Lucifer. It was fun for me to elaborate on events from the past that have previously been alluded to in the Sam Spallucci books.

I guess that Child of Light, like so many of my stories, had its initial seeds way back in my teenage years. I was not a very happy teen. Things were tense at home: little money, an ill father and arguing parents. Consequently, one day, I simply decided that I'd had enough. I remember it being a warm summer's day when I walked out of our front door with no intention of going back. I didn't take anything with me. All I had was just the clothes on my back and the trainers on my feet.

I didn't get very far.

I must have gotten about three or four miles out of town when I realised that I was knackered, turned around and hitched a ride back into town. I remember the guy who gave me a lift being a very *chill dude*. He asked me

Child of Light

what I was doing and I replied that I was just out for a walk.

"Anywhere in particular?" he inquired.

"Not really," I said.

He just nodded and drove me back into town.

I went home, let myself in and headed up to my room.

My parents didn't even realise that I'd left the house.

A few years later, the memory of that day came back to me and I sat down to write a novel about it called *No Fixed Abode*. It was going to be a grand coming-of-age affair. Our hero would run away from his parents, have a relationship with an older woman (who would turn out to be decidedly crazy) and there would be a group of Gypsies. I wasn't sure what I was going to do with the Gypsies, but I knew that the story needed them.

I think I wrote about four pages.

And so it sat languishing in a filing cabinet drawer on a few faded sheets of A4 typed manuscript for about twenty years or so. Then, when I sat down and started writing the Sam Spallucci stories, it called out to me from its creative purgatory. I knew from the word go that I wanted to write a backstory for the mysterious Alec, just as I did with the vampire Nightingale in *Songbird*. So, I turned to the idea of *No Fixed Abode*. The first thing I had to do was, well, start again.

Completely.

I sketched out the first scene where Lucifer is telling him to kill his parents, felt satisfied with that and left it for another ten years.

Back into the filing cabinet it went.

Then, as *Lux Æterna* drew closer and closer, I realised that I would need to explore the stories of the Twins. Amanda's story had suffered a similar fate to Alec's. That one had started out as my take on a *Point Horror* story which I had entitled *Halfling*. So, in 2021, I began to plot both stories with more method and effort. Within a short while, I had the plots for *Child of Light* and *Child of Fire*.

I had initially wanted to publish them both as a single-volume *duology* (as Sam often says, my word, I'm claiming it…) or, at the very least, a pair of novellas. However, time got away from me or, more precisely, the beast that was *Lux Æterna*. As a result, I decided to focus on *Child of Light,* leaving *Child of Fire* to be written later as an accompaniment to the penultimate Sam Spallucci adventure, *Dare The Dragon*.

It has been great fun but exceedingly hard work writing *Child of Light*. For a small work, it has taken an inordinate amount of time. Not only has there been a lot of research involved (especially regarding Davidic and Solomonic Jerusalem) but also, I have been constantly going over older books of mine to make sure that things match up. In *Troubled Souls,* there is a reference that Alec makes about things his mother has done which is still somewhat of a loose end, but I know how to tie that one up in *Child of Fire* and *Dare The Dragon*. There are times when it's a great advantage to have a character who is a psychic.

For me, the highlight of writing this novella has been spending far more quality time with Lucifer. He is such a great character to work with. His knowing looks, his snappy one-liners and his cool dress sense combine to create a fantastic literary creation. Alongside that, his interactions with the likes of Asmodeus and Asherah were an utter hoot to play with and I think the segment in Israel is probably my favourite part of the book. This is, I suppose, in part because I've been chomping at the bit to get the building of the Temple all typed up as it's been banging around in my head for many years now. I feel that I've done a good job of fleshing out the character who will really come into his own in *Lux Æterna*. I hope that you agree.

Anyway, I'll tootle off now and leave you to it. I hope that this novella has answered certain questions as well as having posed others. Please let me know what you think about it, and any theories that you might have, over on social media.

Take care and keep looking for what lurks in the shadows.

ASC September 2024.

About The Author

A.S.Chambers resides in Lancaster, England. He lives a fairly simple life of walking in the countryside, gazing at mountains and wondering if clouds taste of candy-floss.

He is quite happy for, and in fact would encourage, you to follow him on Facebook, Instagram, Threads, TikTok, Patreon and YouTube.

There is also a nice, shiny website:
www.aschambers.co.uk

Milton Keynes UK
Ingram Content Group UK Ltd.
UKHW020754231024
450026UK00001B/30